WHEN WE BEGAN

A RIDGEWATER HIGH NOVELLA

WHEN WE
began

JUDY CORRY

ALSO BY JUDY CORRY

Ridgewater High Series:

When We Began (Cassie and Liam)

Meet Me There (Ashlyn and Luke)

Don't Forget Me (Eliana and Jess)

It Was Always You (Lexi and Noah)

My Second Chance (Juliette and Easton)

My Mistletoe Mix-Up (Raven and Logan)

Forever Yours (Alyssa and Jace)

Protect My Heart (Emma and Arie)

The Billionaire Bachelor (Kate and Drew)

Kissing The Boy Next Door (Wes and Lauren)

1

CASSIE

"SEE YOU IN A WEEK, SWEETIE," my mom said through the rolled-down window of her Prius.

"Have fun on your trip." I bent over to see her and Isaac one last time before they went on their anniversary trip to Belize. Then I pulled on the handle of my suitcase and waited until my parents pulled away from the curb before heading up the Turner's driveway to knock on their front door.

Alyssa Turner, one of my best friends, opened the door. Her blue eyes were bright with excitement, her honey-blonde hair pulled up into the ponytail she'd worn to cheerleading practice this morning.

"Cassie! You're here!" Alyssa beckoned me in. "I'm so excited for this week!"

I lifted my suitcase over the threshold and stepped inside. "Me too."

My mom and Isaac had gotten married six years ago, and every year since, they would go on a week-long anniversary trip—which meant that I got to hang out at the Turner's house while they were away.

"I have a surprise," Alyssa said in a sing-song voice.

"Did the football team decide to have an extra summer camp, forcing Liam to be gone all week?" Liam was her older brother who found joy in tormenting me every time I was around him. Power-complex, anyone?

"You wish." Alyssa smiled. "It's something even better."

I didn't know if anything could be better than that dream of mine. For some reason, back in middle school Liam had decided that because I was friends with Alyssa, it also meant that he should take on the role of an honorary big brother. Apparently, bossing around Alyssa and their younger brother Caleb wasn't enough for him.

"My surprise is this way." Alyssa led me from the entryway through the living room and to the hall that led to the bedrooms on the main floor. She stopped by her room at the end of the hall.

"Are you ready?" she asked.

"As ready as I'll ever be." I grinned, having no idea what her surprise was. Alyssa was pretty down to earth usually, so I doubted there was anything crazy waiting behind the door.

She turned the knob and swung the door wide open.

I looked around at her gymnastics trophies and at the photos of us with our friend Raven and Alyssa's boyfriend Trey, which were stuck all over the walls, and tried to figure out what her surprise might be. But her room looked about the same as usual, if not slightly cleaner.

I stepped deeper inside, and then I saw something new. There was an air mattress at the foot of her bed.

"Is that air mattress for me?" I asked.

She looked at me with bright eyes. "Yep, no sleeping pad on the carpet for you this summer, my dear."

"Man, talk about living like a queen." I laughed. "Though I must say that I'm most excited that your bathroom isn't being remodeled anymore. That will be super nice."

"I know, right?" Alyssa sat on her bed. "No more rushing across the hall in my bathrobe anymore."

At the mention of a robe, I couldn't help but remember what had happened the last time I'd stayed over. I'd taken a shower one morning but had forgotten to bring mine. So I had to wrap myself in a towel before going back into Alyssa's room to get dressed. Unfortunately, I'd neglected to poke my head out the door to make sure the coast was clear and ended up running smack into Liam.

Thankfully, I had a good grip on my towel and nothing too awkward happened. But Liam had looked at me differently for the rest of the day.

I set my suitcase against the wall, beneath her window, and saw that Liam was in the backyard, mowing the lawn without a shirt.

I studied his tall frame as he pushed the mower down a stretch of grass. He'd gotten his blond hair cut since the last time I'd seen him. He was wearing dark sunglasses to shade his blue eyes from the sun, and the morning light glistened on his tanned shoulders.

But those weren't the things I noticed most about him.

I'd heard he was going to be the quarterback for Ridgewater High's football team this year, but I hadn't realized how much bigger he'd gotten in the past couple of months to accomplish that.

"Since when did Liam get muscles?" I asked Alyssa, letting my gaze linger on her brother a little longer. Even though I couldn't stand him most of the time, I couldn't deny that he was extremely attractive.

"He's been lifting at the gym with the football team in the mornings." She shrugged and plopped down on her bed. "Not that I've noticed any difference. I *am* his sister."

I pulled my gaze away from the window and shrugged like I hadn't just been checking out her brother. "He looks good."

When I turned to Alyssa, her mouth was hanging open as if I had just said that I saw a pixie flying around back there.

"Did you just compliment my brother?" she asked. "I think I need to write this moment down or something."

I waved my hand and unzipped my suitcase, pulling out my makeup bag. "You say that as if I've never had a nice thing to say about Liam before."

"I don't think you have," she said, her blue eyes still wide with surprise. "Does this mean you two might actually get along with each other instead of acting like a couple of toddlers fighting over a toy all week?"

I unzipped my gold-and-blue makeup case and gave her a noncommittal shrug. "I guess you never know."

"Good. Because Caleb is at science camp all week, and therefore, won't be home to distract Liam. We might have to put up with him more than usual." Caleb was their ten-year-old brother who got into all sorts of mischief when he was around. He was basically just like Liam had been at that age, so I couldn't pretend like I wasn't relieved that at least one of Alyssa's annoying brothers would be gone for the week.

"Liam still has football practice, right? Like, he won't be around twenty-four seven, will he?"

"Yeah, he's usually still at football practice by the time we get home from cheer practice."

"Well, as long as we get a bit of a reprieve, we might be okay." I winked. "What's the plan for today, anyway?"

"Liam and I are watching our nephew Mason today, since his regular babysitter is sick, so we were thinking about taking him to the swimming pool. Does that sound okay?"

"Sure, I can lie in the sun and tan at the pool just as easily as I can in your backyard. Plus, I heard there might be a hot lifeguard there worth checking out." It had been two weeks since Jess Brooks and I had broken up, so it was about time I found a replacement boyfriend. He probably already had a new girlfriend by now with the rate he went through them.

Until dating him myself, I'd always wondered why he went through girls so fast. But after seeing the way he looked at his best friend, I finally understood it. It was obvious he was in love with her, but she was oblivious to it all.

Alyssa spoke, taking me away from my thoughts of my ex. "You do know you don't always have to have a boyfriend, right?"

"Says the girl who's been dating the same guy for a year." I smirked at her then ran some mascara along my lashes.

"Yeah, yeah." Alyssa rolled her eyes.

Alyssa and her boyfriend had been together for seemingly forever, though I still didn't understand why exactly. Alyssa was gorgeous and could have any guy she wanted, and while her boyfriend was nice enough, I couldn't help but think that she only settled because the boy she really liked had moved to North Carolina last summer.

"Why are you putting mascara on before we go swimming?" Alyssa asked.

I pumped my mascara applicator in the tube.

"*You're* going to the pool to swim. *I'm* going to the pool to find a new guy."

"I think you're just too scared to get in the pool after watching that documentary on swimming in public pools last month."

I shrugged. "I've been enlightened and don't have the ability to ignore what I've learned."

"You're not going to catch an infectious disease by going in the pool. That's what all the chlorine is for."

I scrunched up my nose as I brushed another coat of mascara along my lashes. "Yeah, but I don't like thinking about *why* they need to dump all the chlorine in there in the first place."

"DO you want to take him for the first or second half?" Liam, in his deep voice, asked Alyssa as he lifted their nephew Mason from his car seat in the back of Liam's car.

Mason was such a cute toddler. He had big, blue eyes—the same color as all of the Turner siblings—and his dark hair was super curly like his mom's. Of the four siblings, Charlotte Turner was the oldest and had married young and had a kid soon after.

"How about you take him first?" Alyssa said. "That will give me time to wear Cassie down the first half and maybe get her to climb in the disease-infested pool with us."

Liam turned to me as we approached the Ridge-water Aquatic Center. "Charlotte said she already changed a poopy diaper today, so I doubt Mason will leave any chocolate-covered raisins this time around."

I shook my head as images from last summer flashed through my mind. "You just have to bring that up again, don't you?"

Last time we'd taken Mason to the pool, I'd helped Alyssa give him his bath after we'd finished swimming, only to realize too late that he'd pooped in his diaper while we'd swam. And because poop was gross, I'd totally screamed when little balls fell to the ground and at my feet.

Liam, of course, had thought that seeing me jumping up and screaming was the funniest thing in the world. And had been absolutely no help in cleaning Mason up.

"It *was* pretty funny." Liam laughed and held open the door to the Aquatic Center for us. "You have to admit that."

I stepped right next to him and Mason, taking the toddler's hand in mine. "Make sure to poop really good this time, okay? Uncle Liam needs a taste of his own medicine."

Mason smiled at me and said, "Poop," and then laughed his cute two-year-old laugh.

Liam looked down at his nephew. "No poop allowed, Mason."

"Poop." Mason laughed again.

I touched his cute chubby cheeks. "Just save the excitement for Uncle Liam and we'll be best friends forever, okay, little guy?"

Mason flashed a toothy grin and said, "Poop."

I smiled back, deciding we'd come to an agreement, and then continued past the boys and through the door Liam still held open for me.

After paying and getting our wristbands for the day, Alyssa and I took Mason into the locker room with us. I changed into my bathing suit—a cute white two-piece with a lacy overlay—while Alyssa changed Mason into his swim diaper, swim trunks, and life vest.

"Do you mind taking him out to Liam while I change?" Alyssa asked once Mason was ready.

"Sure." I grabbed the beach bag from the bench and took him out to the kiddie pool. Liam was standing with his feet in the water, his light blue swim trunks hanging low on his hips.

Dang, he was looking way better than he should if I wanted to ignore him like I usually did.

I looked down at myself, feeling self-conscious for the first time in front of Liam. My swimsuit was really cute and only showed a few inches of my stomach, but I suddenly wished I hadn't pigged out so much at lunch. I sucked my stomach in before I put Mason down, hoping my food baby wasn't too prominent.

"Well, I'll let you two have your fun," I said. "There's a lounge chair calling my name outside."

Liam took Mason's hand from mine, his fingers grazing my skin briefly in the exchange.

Instead of thinking about the zing of electricity the short touch had shot through my arm, I focused on maintaining a serene expression. And when I looked at Liam again, I caught him running his gaze over the full length of my body before he turned back to his nephew.

Was Liam checking me out?

Liam cleared his throat when he saw that I'd noticed his inspection. After hesitating for a moment, he said, "Don't get too comfortable in your lounge chair. I have a feeling the swimming pool will be calling your name today."

And then he winked.

He'd never winked at me before. Should I be reading into this?

No, it probably wasn't a flirtatious wink, more of a warning wink, like he had some sort of mischief planned.

"I'll make sure to keep an eye out for you in case you decide to try and throw me in."

His eyes lit up. "What a great idea you just gave me."

I gripped my beach bag. "Don't even think about it. Revenge is kind of my thing."

He smiled at me like I'd just presented him with an irresistible challenge. "I'll look forward to it."

2

CASSIE

"YOU SURE you don't want to get in?" Alyssa asked from the deep end of the outdoor pool after she'd just jumped off the diving board.

I held up my gossip magazine. "No, I'm good."

"Suit yourself." She pushed off the side and dove back into the water.

My mom had always called me her little fish when I was younger, since swimming at the pool all day was all I ever wanted to do in the summer when I wasn't playing basketball with my biological dad. But that documentary, combined with my love of hot guys and always wanting to look my best around them, had shifted my love of swimming into a love of tanning.

Sunbathing was exactly how I'd hooked my

summer boyfriend last year, so if I stuck to my plans today it wouldn't be long before I'd find someone new.

A few minutes later, Liam walked outside with Mason, probably having gotten bored in the kiddie pool.

I watched as he slowly stepped into the pool and down the steps. Mason had his arms wrapped tightly around his uncle's neck as they slowly sunk lower into the water. I had to smile. Even though I could barely stand the guy, I had to admit that Liam was really good with his nephew. Most guys didn't seem to know how to hold a baby, but Liam was practically the baby whisperer when Mason was having a bad day.

I would bet that so many girls at school would swoon even more at the mysterious Liam Turner if they got to see this side of him.

Liam waded over to where Alyssa was and handed Mason off to her once she'd reached the shallow end where her feet could touch the bottom. Then he swam under the rope that marked where the deep end started and pulled himself up the steps to line up for the diving board.

I watched him as he stood shivering in the slight breeze. I let my gaze follow him across the board and waited to see which trick he'd do this time. He stood backwards on it, and after getting a good bounce going, he did a backflip into the water. His head broke the surface a moment later.

After swimming back to the pool wall, he slicked his light hair back with his hands. And I couldn't be sure, but it almost sounded like there were angels singing as he pulled himself from the water again.

I shook my head. What was happening to me today?

I'd spent the last few years constantly fighting with him, and now, after one day of seeing him be so cute with his nephew and watching him do a simple trick off the diving board, I was suddenly going gaga over him?

I blinked my eyes and forced my gaze back to my magazine. There was only one explanation for this. I hadn't kissed a guy since Jess and I had broken up, and I was going through withdrawals.

I needed to go find that hot lifeguard to get my hormones pointed in the right direction again. Because having feelings for my friend's brother was the last thing I needed.

But when I scanned the perimeter of the pool for the lifeguards, all I saw were girls from the swim team at school.

I turned a page in my magazine. There was an article about the teen heartthrob, Ky Miller. He was easy on the eyes, so I decided he'd just have to do for now.

I was in the middle of reading the gossip about his most recent girlfriend when I was suddenly lifted into the air and thrown into the pool. A shock of cold water attacked me, and before I knew it, I was sputtering and grasping around for the rim.

I pushed my hair out of my eyes, and once I was able to see, I saw Liam laughing, with his hands on his hips and head thrown back.

"You jerk!" I yelled, splashing water in his direction.

When he just continued laughing at me, I reached up to grab his leg, hoping to pull him into the pool with me. But he stepped back out of my reach.

He took a few more steps back before he started running forward, yelling the word, "Cannonball!"

He hit the surface and a big splash of water assaulted my eyes again.

It was just like fifth grade all over again.

I pushed myself off the rim and swam toward him. Just as his head broke through the surface, I pushed on his shoulders with as much force as I could.

He wasn't expecting my move so he went under easily. But I knew what I did was a bad idea, because once he resurfaced, there was an impish look on his face.

I quickly turned to swim away.

"Oh no, you don't." He grabbed my waist from behind, his grip strong, and pulled me back under the water with him.

We both came up coughing, my nose stinging from the water that had gone in.

"Okay, Liam. That's enough *fun*." I swiped at my eyes and pushed my hair back out of my face as I treaded water.

Liam just stood there like it was the easiest thing in the world to stand in water that was over five feet deep.

Dang you, tall person.

Being average height really did have its limitations.

"You getting tired?" His eyes smiled.

"You think?" Treading water was exhausting.

He stepped closer.

Unsure of what he planned to do next, and not

wanting to find myself dunked underwater, I said, "Truce?"

He narrowed his gaze at me for a moment, seeming to read my face for any signs of lying.

My arms were getting tired, but finally, after another long ten seconds of treading water, Liam said, "Truce."

Then he scooped me up and cradled me in his arms. His unexpected touch did funny things to my insides, but I put one arm around his shoulders as he slowly walked me back closer to the wall.

"Do you want me to carry you all the way back to your chair?" Liam asked.

"It only seems fair, since you're the reason I left it in the first place."

He grinned. "But you have to admit that it was fun, right?" He weaved his way through a bunch of boys playing water basketball.

"Dunking you under was probably the most fun," I allowed.

He pretended to tip me backwards for a second.

"Don't you dare," I yelped and gripped onto his shoulder tighter.

He laughed, his chest rumbling against my side. When did his voice get so deep?

"I'm just joking, Nessie."

"Nessie?"

"You know, like the Loch Ness monster." He said it as if that would make more sense.

"Why would you call me the Loch Ness monster?"

His lips quirked up into a half-smile. "Because you, um, have mascara running down your face and look like something that just resurfaced from the black lagoon."

Ah, of course.

"Well, if I'd known I was going to actually end up in the pool today, I would have worn waterproof." I wiped under my eyes. "Is that better?"

He inspected my face, and I was suddenly aware of just how close we were to each other.

"It's better," he said, his eyes still studying my face.

I tried not to notice how amazing his deep blue eyes looked reflected against the blue water.

I needed to look away. I should actually peel myself away from him and out of his arms. But before I could make myself pull away from him, his expression softened. He said, "You don't always have to wear makeup in public, you know."

My eyebrows knitted together. Why did he just say that?

It didn't matter why. I lengthened my neck. "I don't think you should care about how much makeup I may or may not choose to wear."

And before I could stop it, the memory of the Carmichael twins' party back in eighth grade, when I'd been alone with Liam in a closet for Seven Minutes of Heaven, came to mind—the day I'd thought he was going to kiss me, only to have him lean in and tell me that the thought of kissing his sister's best friend was about as desirable as kissing his sister.

I had never crushed on him, so it shouldn't have hurt as badly as it had. But rejection from a guy was still rejection. And after everything that had already happened with my bio dad, I'd vowed after that day to show Liam just how desirable I could be to other guys and rub it in his face every chance I had. So instead of wearing a ponytail every day and playing sports like softball and basketball, I'd joined Alyssa and Raven in their love of cheerleading and tried out for the cheer team before freshman year.

I'd done everything to change my tomboy persona that had so disgusted him that day in the closet, learning everything I could from video tutorials and magazines about hair and makeup.

And since then, I'd never let him see me looking

anything but my best—well, until just now in the pool with the mascara dripping down my face.

But of course, he had to comment on my makeup. There was always something wrong with me in Liam's eyes. Just like I hadn't been good enough for my bio dad to stick around.

We reached the steps that led out of the pool, and I let go of him. "I think I can walk the rest of the way."

He released his hold. As soon as my feet touched the pool floor, I climbed onto the first step, ready to put some distance between us. But then, not wanting him to know that his comments on my makeup had any effect on me, I turned around and said, "You know I'm going to get you back for this, right?" I gestured to indicate how I was now wet instead of dry.

He smiled, and I was grateful he didn't seem to know that he'd offended me. "I look forward to seeing you try."

3

LIAM

"YOU ABOUT READY TO LEAVE?" I sat in the lounge chair beside Cassie about thirty minutes after I'd thrown her into the pool.

Cassie turned a page in her gossip magazine whose cover boasted *50 Ways to Get Ready Faster* and *Five Ways to Make Your Lips More Kissable*.

If I had to describe Cassie to anyone using only six words, they would be "high-maintenance," "obsessed with guys," and "chameleon." She was so busy trying to be the *perfect* girl—what she thought guys wanted—that I didn't think she knew who she really was.

Her eyes skimmed over the rest of whatever article she was reading for a moment longer, and then she closed her magazine around her finger. "I'm ready whenever you guys are."

"And what new beauty tip are you going to try today?" I asked, nodding at her magazine.

She gave me an annoyed look. "You can make fun of it all you want, Liam, but these things work. I started dating Jess Brooks after the issue about the pink makeup trend. And Jake Haley always loved how shiny and soft my hair was when we dated—for which I have last November's issue of this magazine to thank."

I wanted to laugh at how brainwashed she was by this stuff but decided to go along with it instead. "So, what did you learn about making your lips more kissable? I know that's the article you read first."

She huffed and set her feet on the ground, readying to stand. "Nothing I didn't know already— as any of my ex-boyfriends would be able to tell you, if you asked. My nightly routine includes lip care, of course."

"Of course," I said sarcastically.

She was always quick to tell me how many ex-boyfriends she had. She never seemed to care about the word "ex," though. And I couldn't help but think that the reason they were exes was because she never let them get to know the real Cassie. But then again, I've known her since elementary and I still wasn't sure I knew exactly who she was, either. She'd changed so much over the past few years, and sadly, I'd liked the old version of Cassie better. At least back before she cared so much about how she looked, she'd been fun.

We rounded up Alyssa and Mason a few minutes later and went out to my car. I was just wrestling Mason into his car seat when Cassie spoke from behind me.

"Is that Luke Davenport?"

I looked up to see what Cassie was talking about. Sure enough, running down the sidewalk was Luke, one of the football co-captains.

"I think I found my next guy," Cassie said. The excitement in her voice was hard to miss.

"More like victim," I muttered.

"Shut up, Liam." She whacked me on the shoulder before turning around to wave at Luke.

I went back to strapping Mason in the rest of the way. Mason hated his car seat and was doing every-thing he could to get out of it, arching his back and turning from side to side. When I was finally done and he was sufficiently trapped, I climbed in the

driver seat and turned on the air conditioning—
having worked up a sweat in my wrestling match.

Alyssa climbed into the passenger side.

"Where's Cassie?" I turned to my sister as she
buckled in beside me.

"You heard her. Luke is her next guy." Alyssa
gestured down the sidewalk. "She went to get him."

I leaned my head back against the headrest and
watched Cassie flirt with Luke, who was jogging in
place like he was somewhat agitated. His mom had
just died from cancer last month, and from what I'd
seen of him at football camp, he was having a really
hard time with it.

"How much do you wanna bet that she comes
back here and asks me everything I know about football?" I asked.

That was how it always was with her. If her
boyfriend liked skateboarding, she liked skateboarding. If he was into art, Cassie was into art. If he liked
video games, she was asking me all about the latest
game and watching me while I played—annoying me
with questions about who the characters were and
what their goals were for the game. She even took
detailed notes so she could memorize all the
information.

I was all for trying new things to see if you liked them, but trying new things was like a full-time job for Cassie.

Alyssa was watching her as well. "I don't really want to bet against you because I'm pretty sure she's gonna try to find a way to become the football team's water girl *and* still cheer at your games after this."

I watched Cassie a little longer. She was grinning broadly up at Luke, gesturing to his running shoes. After a few minutes, she waved her fingers at him and he continued his run.

When she got back to my car, I had to come out to let her in, since the seat on the other side of Mason was already filled with the beach bag Alyssa had placed back there.

"So when is Luke taking you out?" I asked Cassie as I pushed my seat forward for her.

"No date yet. But he did tell me about a party in the north woods tomorrow night. He said a bunch of other kids from school will be there."

"Yeah, I heard about it," I said.

"Are you going?" she asked as she climbed in.

"I was thinking about it." It would be good to see everyone again before school started next week.

"We should go together then. I'm sure Alyssa and

Trey would like to come, too." She glanced at Alyssa as she buckled her seatbelt. "Right, Alyssa?"

Alyssa shrugged like she was open to the idea. "I'm in. I'm sure Raven would love to come, too."

I sighed and pushed my seat back into position. "I guess we can all go together. Just don't complain to me if Luke doesn't ask you out."

"What makes you think he won't ask me out?" Cassie asked, pouting her full bottom lip.

I sunk down into my seat and shut the door. "If he didn't ask you out after all the flirting you just did, I don't know how going to a party will change his mind."

I really doubted he was ready to start dating anyone right now. He hadn't been very open to talking about his mom's death with anyone on the football team. But since we'd shared a room at football camp, I'd been there to witness one of his panic attacks in the middle of the night.

Someone dealing with that kind of grief most likely wasn't in a place to date someone like Cassie.

But Cassie didn't seem to hear me because she said, "Well, since someone thought it would be fun to throw me into the pool, Luke probably forgot what I looked like all done up. You just wait, I bet he won't be able to keep his eyes off me tomorrow night."

I started the engine instead of telling her that she was way too obsessed with her looks. Sure she was gorgeous, even I had to admit that. But she relied on her looks too much and didn't seem to realize that some guys actually cared about a girl's personality, too.

Back before she changed so much, I had a huge crush on her. Such a big crush that once, at a party, I'd arranged with my buddy Logan to pick her to be my partner in Seven Minutes of Heaven. I'd almost kissed her that day...until I freaked out when I realized I'd never kissed a girl before and had no idea what I was supposed to do.

So, instead of manning up and admitting to her I'd never done this before, like an idiot I'd said that kissing her would be like kissing my sister—a sentence I'd regretted ever since.

I always wondered if her sudden obsession with impressing guys had to do with what had happened, but I'd never gotten up the nerve to apologize to her. If I told her that I'd messed up because I'd been nervous about kissing her, she'd know about my pathetic crush and probably be weirded out. Because until that day, she'd only ever seen me as the guy who would sometimes shoot hoops with her in our backyard when Alyssa was stuck doing a chore.

But at least by rejecting her first she hadn't been able to reject me.

I was stupid. Back then, my ego wouldn't have been able to take it—not that it would be able to take it now, either, which was why I only ever got up the nerve to ask a girl out until after I was completely sure I wasn't going to be turned down.

Since then, I'd been trying to let her know in little ways that she didn't need to worry so much about everything. Like telling her she didn't need makeup in the pool.

Only those comments never seemed to work like I wanted. They only seemed to make her mad at me.

Cassie was a confusing girl.

And since I knew that the Cassie who was with me today was caused by my own stupid words, I said, "Just act like yourself and that will give you your best chance."

She made a face in the rearview mirror. "Thanks for the brotherly advice, Liam. But I think I know what I'm doing."

Oh well. I tried.

As we pulled onto the road, I tried to think about something else.

Because Cassie may be obsessed with guys, but she also had a side to her that was endearing.

At least, I was pretty sure the old Cassie was still in there somewhere.

WHEN WE GOT BACK to the house, Cassie pulled Mason out of his car seat and held him out to me. "It's your turn to take care of him this time."

I took him from her. "Fine by me. Mason and I are buds."

She seemed like she was holding back a smile as we walked back into the house, but I had no idea why.

"Ready for your bath?" I asked Mason as I placed him in the tub.

"Bubbles. Bubbles." Mason nodded enthusiastically.

"Okay, lots of bubbles. But first we have to take off your swim trunks and swim diaper."

"Otay," he said, standing there with his little chubby hands clasped together.

I ruffled his hair with my hand. He really was the cutest little guy.

I pulled his green-and-blue striped swim trunks down, laying them over the side of the tub. But when I pulled the dinosaur swim diaper down, I noticed—

too late—that Mason had left a little surprise for me. It plopped out and fell at his feet.

How did I not smell that?

"Oh no, Mason. Don't do this to me," I complained at the mess I was going to have to deal with. "I thought we were buddies."

Mason's happy demeanor changed once he saw what was at his feet, and he immediately started screaming and trying to climb out of the tub.

What was I supposed to do?

If I stopped to clean up the mess, Mason would run away and get poop everywhere.

"Can someone help me in here?" I called out the open door. "Please!"

A moment later, Cassie came around the corner in her swim top and shorts, laughing.

"Did Mason do it to you, too, then?" she asked through her giggles.

She didn't look nearly as surprised as I thought she should be.

I narrowed my gaze. "Did you know this was in here? Is that why you handed him to me?"

She leaned against the doorframe with a purple popsicle in hand. "It's only fair after last year."

Mason was about to fall out of the tub in his

desperation to get away from his own mess. I grabbed him before he could fall.

"Will you hold him for me while I take care of the poop?"

She shook her head. "You didn't help me out last year. I think it's only fair for me to sit out and watch this time."

I gestured at my nephew. "I can't console him and clean up at the same time."

"Fine." She sighed and grabbed the towel on the towel rack. "I'll take him, but only because I care about Mason."

I quickly sprayed him off with the handheld shower head. When Mason looked clean enough, Cassie opened the towel for him, wrapping it around his lower half before nuzzling him against her chest to comfort him.

"Thank you," I said.

"You're welcome." Then in a quieter voice, she whispered, "Good job, Mason. I think we're going to be best friends after all."

"Don't listen to her, Mason. She's pure evil."

Cassie shook her head. "You know who's the best, don't you, Mason?" she cooed, looking at me from the corner of her brown eyes as she let him suck on her grape popsicle.

I just shook my head and turned back to the tub, trying to figure out the best way to deal with the mess.

"You're lucky it's all contained in the tub," Cassie said from behind me. "When it happened to me and Alyssa last year, we had those little raisins all over the floor in here."

"I feel so lucky," I said sarcastically. "At least when it happened to you it was a surprise to *all* of us. But this time, *you* actually knew about it beforehand and could have warned me."

When she didn't say anything else, I got to work cleaning up the mess. Once everything was all disinfected, I filled the tub with water and bubbles and took Mason back from Cassie.

"Are you happier now?" I asked Mason who seemed way calmer now that he had the purple popsicle ring around his lips.

"Uh-huh." He nodded and grabbed the toys we had in a mesh bag suctioned to the tub. While he played, I sat down on the closed toilet seat and turned to Cassie who was still standing by the door.

"I think you can count that as revenge for me throwing you in the pool today, okay?" I said.

She shook her head as she sucked on her popsicle. "No, that was revenge for last year. I still have plans to get you back for today."

I shook my head and smiled despite myself. "Good luck with that."

She tried every summer to pull some kind of prank on me. It never worked, but it was fun to watch her try. And in its own weird way, it was kind of like having the real Cassie back when she was trying to get even with me.

4

CASSIE

"ARE you really going to try and get Liam back for throwing you in the pool?" Alyssa asked later that night as we got ready for bed in her room. "Wasn't Mason pooping for him enough karma for the day?"

I fluffed my pillow and set it at one end of the air mattress. "It's the principle of the matter. If he thinks he can get away with that, what else will he try this week?"

"So what are you going to do?"

I grabbed my pajamas out of my suitcase. "I was thinking of trying the old shaving-cream trick."

"What trick is that?"

"It's where you sneak up on someone who is sleeping and put a bunch of shaving cream on their hand. Then when they scratch their face or rub their eyes, which most people do at least sometime during the night, they'll get a face full of shaving cream."

It wasn't the worst thing I could think of doing, but it would be fun. And it would show Liam that he couldn't just tease me all week long and not get any sort of payback for it.

Alyssa laughed as she walked into her bathroom. "Well, don't come crying to me when he inevitably ends up making things worse for you instead."

I followed her and set my bathroom kit on the counter. "If he's as deep a sleeper as you are, I don't think that will be a problem."

She shrugged as she put toothpaste on her toothbrush. "Whatever you say."

I splashed my face with water and squeezed a dime-size amount of face wash onto my finger. "Does your brother have something against makeup?"

Alyssa frowned in confusion. She spit her toothpaste out and wiped her mouth dry with the back of her hand. "I don't think so, why?"

I shrugged as I spread the face wash on my forehead. "I don't know. Just something Liam said today made me wonder about it."

"What did he say?"

"That I don't have to wear makeup all the time."

"Maybe he just remembers what you looked like

when you didn't wear it, and he liked that."

"Well, that would just be weird." I bent over the sink and rinsed off my face. I looked way better with makeup. "Anyway, do you want me to wake you up when I go do my shaving-cream prank?" I grabbed the hand towel I'd gotten from their hall closet and patted my face dry.

"I'll let you do that one on your own. I'm quite partial to sleep and we have cheer practice early in the morning. Feel free to tell me how it goes, though."

"Oh, I will." I smiled just thinking about it. "Though I'm sure Liam will let us know first thing when he storms up the stairs tomorrow morning."

I pulled my shaving cream out of my suitcase and set it by my air mattress before climbing in and pretending to sleep for the night.

Alyssa was dead to the world about ten minutes later, and I just stared at the ceiling, waiting for the minutes to tick by. I hoped Liam was as deep a sleeper as Alyssa was and that he also fell asleep just as fast.

Sleeping habits had to be hereditary, right?

I checked the time on my phone after what seemed like forever. It had only been about thirty minutes since Liam had told everyone he was heading to bed. But that was enough time, right?

After waiting a few more minutes, I grabbed my Island Berry Breeze scented shaving cream and tiptoed out of Alyssa's room. The hall was quiet, and the house was dark when I opened the door. All good signs.

I tiptoed down the hall and down the stairs, my stomach flipping at the thought of what Mr. and Mrs. Turner might do if they found me sneaking down to their son's room.

But I tried to push those thoughts away, because I wasn't doing anything like that. I was just getting the revenge I had promised Liam to expect.

Liam's room was at the end of the hall, past the bathroom and the storage room that they had down there. The lights were all off, and his door was open, showing that his room was dark as well.

I smiled to myself as my heart pounded with anticipation. Growing up, I didn't have any siblings to play tricks on, so this was my only way to get my fix. Even if he didn't give me the reaction I was hoping for, just this experience in and of itself was exhilarating.

I peeked my head through the doorway and found that he was indeed already asleep in his bed. I sighed a breath of relief and tried to figure out the path I would take to get to him. His floor was surprisingly clean. I'd always known a relationship with a boy wasn't going to last if I saw that his bedroom was a stinky mess. Liam might actually make a great boyfriend to some girl someday.

I shook my head. Why was I thinking about that?

I zeroed back into the scene ahead and decided it was now or never. Getting down on my hands and knees, I crawled across his carpeted floor. Liam was laying on his back with one hand resting on his chest, the other flopped out to the side. I had to hold in another giggle as I got closer.

This is so fun!

I slowly peeked my head up above his mattress and got to a kneeling position. I watched him for a moment to gauge how deep asleep he was. His chest rose and fell rhythmically, and he had a peaceful expression on his face. If he was still just barely drifting off, this wouldn't work.

He didn't twitch or turn after about thirty seconds, so I slowly lifted the can of shaving cream closer to his open hand. I pressed down the button, dispensing purple foam in the center of his palm.

His fingers twitched.

I quickly ducked down by his bed. Did I wake him?

My pulse thundered in my temples as I listened

and held my breath.

Don't wake up. Don't wake up.

When I didn't hear any movements again, I propped myself back up and dispensed more shaving cream onto his palm. I wanted to add a good healthy amount so that it would really have the chance to get all over his face. I leaned a little closer to add my last finishing touches. But before I knew what was happening, his hand was in my face, smearing the shaving cream all over.

I screamed. "Stop, Liam! Stop!" I sputtered when he continued to rub it all over my eyes, nose, and mouth.

His low rumble of laughter greeted my ears as I tried wiping the crap off my face.

"You didn't actually think I was asleep, did you?" he asked, his tone way too happy as he propped himself up on his elbow.

Ugh. I jumped up and stomped out of his bedroom and into his bathroom to wash my face. His footsteps followed closely behind, as he chuckled after me.

"Was this that revenge you warned me about earlier?" He leaned against the doorframe as I splashed my face with water.

"Shut up, Liam."

He laughed again.

The jerk!

I heard the closet door open, and a moment later, he put a small towel in my hand.

"You can use that to dry off."

"How thoughtful of you," I muttered, grudgingly taking it.

When I was done patting my face dry, I tossed the towel back at Liam, more than ready to go upstairs instead of hearing him laugh at me some more.

I was just about to step past him when he stopped me. "You missed a spot."

"Where?" I turned to look at my reflection in the mirror but didn't see any shaving cream left.

What I did see, though, was my makeup-less face.

Yikes! Not my best look.

He stepped closer, and it was then that I realized he wasn't wearing a shirt. I'd been too caught up to notice earlier, when I was making sure he was asleep.

I forced my gaze away from his six pack to look him in the eyes. But that wasn't the greatest idea, either, because I'd always thought his eyes were nice —even if I didn't think the owner of said eyes was the nicest. They always made deranged little butterflies flutter in my stomach. Yes, they were deranged because they should know better than to come to life when I was with Liam.

"You missed a spot right here." He touched the top of my head, and then showed me the small amount of white foam that was on the tip of his finger now.

I smoothed my hands over my face and hair again.

"Is that all of it?" I asked, hoping that by talking I'd stop feeling the strange attraction to him that was coming over me.

He stepped around me to wash his finger off, his chest brushing against my shoulder and making tingles erupt all over my arm.

"Yup. I think that was it."

"Thanks," I managed to say.

"Oh, you are very welcome." He grinned as he dried his hands on the towel that I'd used. "Make sure to let me know the next time you're thinking about getting revenge on me, so I'll be prepared to save you from yourself."

I rolled my eyes and walked out the door. But his words definitely gave me something to think about. He had been way too smug the past five minutes. I needed to find a way to get him back.

5

LIAM

BY THE TIME I got up the next morning, Alyssa and Cassie had already gone to cheerleading practice, so I didn't see Cassie until I got home from football practice just before lunch time.

"Finally, someone is home," Cassie said when I stepped into the living room. She was sitting on the couch with her hair in a high ponytail and she wore a purple shirt with cut-off shorts.

"You're here by yourself?" I looked around. "Where's Alyssa?"

"Trey got back a few days early from his trip to North Carolina and whisked her away." She pointed the remote at the TV to power it off. "So I've just been sitting here, bored out of my mind for the past hour."

"Bored out of your mind?" I raised an eyebrow. "Don't you have some makeup tutorial you could be making?"

She had a whole YouTube channel dedicated to fashion and beauty tips.

Not that I'd watched it.

Well, okay, so I did once, just to see what was all that she could talk about for so many episodes. And though I'd never tell her, since it would only boost her ego even more, there were quite a few guys on the football team who watched her channel just because they thought she was hot.

But she rolled her eyes and said, "That's not all I do all day, you know."

"You have other interests?"

"I have plenty of interests."

I smiled. "Oh, yeah, that's right. Like finding your next boyfriend."

"Well, of course. But as you already know, I'll be focusing on that hobby tonight at the party. But I still have a whole day of just sitting around your house ahead of me."

"How long did Alyssa say she'd be with Trey?"

"She said she'd be back by dinner so we could get ready for the party together."

"Alyssa really just left you here all alone for the

day?" I knew Trey had been gone for two weeks to visit Jace and Logan Carmichael, but they could have taken Cassie along on their date.

At least, not leave her here for me to entertain.

Cassie shrugged, and it looked like she was trying not to feel left behind by my sister. "It's fine. I understand. I'd want to hang out with my boyfriend, too, if I had one right now."

I frowned, and for a moment, a pang of sympathy passed through me.

That was weird. Since when did I feel bad for Cassie?

"So what are your plans for the rest of the day?" Cassie wrapped a piece of hair around her finger. "Are you going to abandon me, too?"

"Since when do you want to hang out with me?"

"Since there's literally no one else around." She gestured at my empty and quiet house. My parents both worked, and with Caleb gone to science camp, I really was the only one left to entertain her.

"Well..." I set my football bag on the ground and walked over to the couch to sit right next to her. I put my arms around her and pulled her next to me just because I knew how much she hated it when I was all sweaty from practice. "I'm so glad you want to hang out with me."

She wrinkled her nose and tried to push me away. "Go take a shower, Liam. You stink and you're getting me all gross."

I just laughed and pulled her even closer. "Do you smell that?"

She pushed on me again. "Yes. And like I said, you stink."

When she started pinching me in the sides—my weak spot—I was forced to release my hold on her.

Free again, she scooted clear over to the other end of the couch.

"You don't have to pretend that you don't like cuddling with me." I crossed my arms. "I know how much you like it."

"Yeah. I just love getting your football sweat all over me after I've just showered."

I sniffed the sleeve of my practice jersey. Yeah, I stunk. But instead of admitting it, I said, "It's not that bad. You're just being overly dramatic."

"You're delusional, but sure, I'll just take that as a compliment. I *have* always thought it would be fun to join the drama club."

"You have?" I never would have guessed it.

"Sure. It would be fun." She scratched at a spot on her shorts like she was suddenly feeling self-conscious. She peeked over at me. "I was actually considering trying out for the spring play this year."

"Well, I guess that makes sense. If you joined the drama department, you could save all your acting for the stage and stop reinventing yourself all the time just to impress a guy."

Oops, did I just say that out loud?

Her jaw dropped and she crossed her arms. "What's that supposed to mean?"

"Nothing..." I hurried to say. And from the fire in her eyes, I could tell that she was *not* happy about what I'd said.

She swiveled on her cushion and faced me. "I promise you that I really don't know what you meant when you said I act like someone different to impress guys."

Yeah, that shouldn't have slipped out. Not if I wanted to live through the afternoon.

I ran a hand through my hair as I tried to figure out how to get out of this.

"Liam?" she pressed. "What did you mean?"

I sighed, knowing she'd just keep pestering me until I explained. "I guess I was saying that it seems like you haven't really been yourself ever since you decided to do cheer instead of sports."

"Cheer is a sport."

"You know what I mean." I shrugged, trying to figure out how to word it. "I guess you just got way more obsessed with fashion and hair and flirting."

She arched her eyebrows. "And is there something wrong with caring about putting my best face forward?"

Well, there was when she wasn't putting forth her real face.

But since saying that would only make her even madder, I sighed and said, "Sometimes, I just miss who you used to be. I don't know. We used to have so much fun back in the day."

"So I've evolved a little. That shouldn't be a big deal." She lifted her hands in the air. "I mean, it's not like you really cared that much about the old me. Is it so bad that I wanted guys to notice me instead of just being one of the guys?"

I punched myself internally. Yep, pretty sure her obsession with impressing guys was my fault.

All because I'd said that one stupid comment because I'd been so nervous.

But since my current way of talking to her about it didn't seem to be working, I decided I needed to change my tactics.

"So, you dated a lot of guys in the past couple of years, right?"

She looked at me warily like she was worried I was going to insult her again. "Yeah."

"And those relationships have only ever lasted for a few weeks, right?"

"There's nothing wrong with dating around."

I held my hands up before she could put up her walls. "I wasn't saying it was bad. I was just wondering if that's what you really want."

I studied her carefully to make sure I wasn't upsetting her any further. When she seemed interested in hearing me out, I continued, "I guess I just wonder if maybe your relationships would last longer if you went about them differently."

"You want to give me dating advice?" she scoffed. "You've been on, like, three dates in the past six months, right?"

"We aren't talking about me right now. We're talking about you."

"What if I want to talk about you instead?" She slumped against the couch and pouted.

I ignored her. "So you really want to have your best chance with Luke tonight, right?"

She glanced away briefly, like she was trying not to look too interested. "Maybe..."

"Well, I was just thinking that you might have a better chance with him if you stopped trying to show guys what you thought they wanted, and just let them get to know the real Cassie—the Cassie who just told me she was interested in being in a play. The Cassie who sneaks into people's rooms at night to try, *and fail,* at getting her revenge on them."

"But guys don't like that kind of stuff. They like their own interests." She frowned. "Believe me, I've dated a lot of them and all they want to talk about is football or video games."

"I'm just saying that by trying to fit into some 'ideal girlfriend mold,' you're not being fair to yourself. You should be more interested in finding a guy who likes you for who you really are."

She pouted. "Well, sporty Cassie never worked very well for anyone."

It worked for me.

"What did you say?" Her eyes widened with shock.

Did I really say those words out loud?

Stupid!

"Nothing, I was just saying that, um..." My mind went completely blank. How did I let that slip?

"You were saying what?" she asked again.

How was I supposed to get out of this?

Then I had an idea. It was probably stupid, but it was the only thing I could think of at the moment.

"I was just saying that we could try my theory out on me. You know, like a test run."

Her eyebrows knit together. "Try what out on you?"

"Well, I was thinking we could go on like a practice date. We can do something fun and date-like, and the only rule will be that you have to say the first thing that comes to your mind, instead of thinking about what you want me to hear while we're out doing whatever. It'll be good practice for tonight when you talk to Luke."

She narrowed her eyes. "You want to go on a practice date with me?"

My palms felt sweaty when I realized I'd just set myself up to be shot down. I couldn't let that happen, so I hurried to say, "Never mind. It was a stupid idea."

But she looked thoughtful. "No, it's not stupid." She paused, as if thinking on it a little more. "I mean, it's not like I have anything else to do today. Sure, let's go do something fun."

"Really?"

She was actually considering going on a practice date with me?

"Sure." She shrugged. "In fact, how about we make it mutually beneficial?"

"'Mutually beneficial?'" What was she suggesting?

"I noticed that you seemed to have a thing for Bridgett Maynard last spring, and with Ryan moving away this summer, she's probably looking for a new boyfriend..."

"And?" I swallowed, really having no idea how helping her with this would help me get Bridgett's attention—not that I had really thought much about Bridgett since summer started.

She played with the end of her ponytail. "Well, since I don't know if I've ever seen you go on a second date with anyone, I just figured that maybe there was something you were doing wrong."

Oh, good. Now I was going to be one of her projects.

But since I was interested to hear what she was going to suggest, I didn't shut her down yet.

She continued, "Anyway, I just figured that if we're pretending this is a date, I could watch you and see what you normally do on dates with girls, and possibly give you some pointers of my own so you can finally get a second date."

"I don't need any help getting a second date. The reason why I haven't been on a second date with a girl in a while is because I haven't been interested in one."

"But don't you like kissing? It's hard to do much of that if you're not going on second dates."

"I do just fine," I muttered. Sure, I may not have kissed that many girls, but the few I had kissed definitely hadn't complained.

She raised her eyebrows like she didn't believe me. "There is always room for improvement."

I rolled my eyes but decided it wasn't worth arguing about, so I said, "Fine, I'll teach you everything I know, and you can teach me everything you know."

"Oh, we're not kissing." She pointed at herself and then to me.

"I promise." That ship had sailed years ago. Sailed far, far away and was probably past Pluto by now.

"Perfect."

With everything decided, I stood. "How about we start this practice date with lunch at Cafe Amore?"

"Sure," she said. Then after giving me a good once-over, she added, "But you need to shower first."

I laughed. "Of course. Just give me a few minutes and I'll be ready for our *date*."

6

CASSIE

"THIS PLACE HAS THE BEST FOOD," I said to Liam when he parked at a little shop in one of the shopping malls downtown.

"Do you come here often?" he asked.

"My grandma and grandpa bring us here every time they visit." I looked at the shop with the sign "Cafe Amore" above it, remembering all the times I'd been here before. The building looked a little rundown on the outside, but the food more than made up for the curb appeal.

We climbed out of his car and walked to the entrance. The bell on the door jingled when Liam opened it for me.

"What a gentleman," I said, praising his already

good behavior. "You wouldn't believe how many guys don't think to open doors for me when we go on dates."

"I don't know why you're so surprised," he said as he followed me inside the cafe. "I'm not the one who said he needed dating tips today."

"Are you telling me it's all in my head, then?" I looked coyly over my shoulder at him.

"Yes." He bent close to my ear and whispered, "But don't worry, once I show you just how good my dating skills actually are, I'll be the only thing inside your head."

Chills rushed over my entire body. Did he really just say that?

To me?

But instead of letting him know that he'd totally just made my body temperature rise a few degrees, I said, "Don't bet on it."

I quickly turned around again to study the menu. I was just reading over the list of sandwiches when I heard him say "challenge accepted" under his breath.

The skin at the back of my neck prickled, and I had to know what he meant by it.

"What do you mean *challenge accepted*?" I craned my neck to look at him.

He crossed his arms over his muscular chest and gave me a too-confident grin. "It just means that I'm going to take this practice date even more seriously now. I'll show you that I can be boyfriend material if I want to be."

Oh, he did, didn't he?

I crossed my arms and fully turned toward him. "There's just one problem with your logic, Liam."

"And what's that?"

"I'm not your average fabric shopper. I take great care in picking out the right material for my boyfriends. It's not just something you can force. It's either there, or it isn't."

"Lucky for you I just happen to be every girl's dream material."

WE ORDERED our food and found a table in the corner. The cafe wasn't too busy, so it only took a few minutes for the waitress to bring me my Philly Cheesesteak sandwich and Liam his Stromboli.

After taking a bite of my delicious sandwich, I wiped my mouth with a napkin and asked, "So what do you have planned next for this date of ours?"

He was about to take a bite of his Stromboli but held his fork mid-air as a confused expression crossed his face. "What?"

"The plans for our practice date," I said. "You made plans, right?"

He set his fork down. "I thought you were making the plans for this."

"You're the one who invited me on this practice date." I shook my head. "I know I said I was going to help you learn how to be better at dating, but I didn't realize you were this clueless."

"I'm not clueless."

I arched an eyebrow. "So you don't usually make your dates plan what you're doing?"

"Of course not." He took a bite of his food. "I usually plan them out way before I get up the nerve to ask a girl."

"Well, that's good, at least," I said. "But we might need to go over proper table manners. Like, how it's rude to speak with your mouth full."

He rolled his eyes and took a sip of his Dr. Pepper. "Sorry," he said after setting his cup back down. "I forgot you were going to be watching my every move. I'm so used to you just ignoring me when we're together."

I might have been reading into things, but did he seem upset that I had better things to do with my time than drool over my friend's older brother when I was at her house?

Well, it wasn't like he hadn't shunned me in the past, either.

I decided to get back to my original question.

"Did you really expect me to come up with the schedule for the day?" I asked.

He shook his head. "No, I was joking when I said that." A half-smile quirked up his lips, and I couldn't help but think that he looked really nice when he smiled. He had great teeth and his lips were perfectly shaped as well.

I wondered how well he knew how to use his lips...

He continued to speak, bringing my thoughts back to the present.

"I was thinking it might be fun to go fishing at Little York Lake today," he said.

"Fishing?" I asked, not feeling too excited about his suggestion.

"It will be fun."

"But I don't know the first thing about fishing." My mom and Isaac never went fishing. My bio dad had taken me maybe a couple of times when I was little, but since he'd chosen to not be in the picture for several years, he certainly hadn't been taking me.

"Then all the more reason for us to do it." Liam smiled. "This way it will be a new thing for you, and you won't have time to study beforehand and learn everything you can about fishing, like you usually do for your dates."

"I don't study before my dates."

"So you've never tried to ask me about a certain video game just because you knew the guy you were interested in was a big-time gamer?" He raised a challenging eyebrow.

"Fine." I picked up my sandwich to take another bite. "So I like to be well-informed. There's nothing wrong with that." It was just me taking my dating life seriously.

He took another sip of his drink. "I think this will be good for you. You can just go with the flow and be in awe of my awesome fisherman's skills."

"Good luck with that. Like I said before, I'm not as easily impressed as you may think."

"Apparently, you have no idea who you're dealing with." He leaned over his plate. "I meant what I said about being the only thing on your mind by the end of this fake date."

It was surprisingly attractive to see this confidence in Liam. I couldn't keep a smile from lifting my cheeks. But since I couldn't let him know that I actually enjoyed seeing this side of him, I said, "The only one who will be wishing this date was real by the end of the day is you."

CASSIE and I grabbed my fishing gear from my garage and stuck it in the trunk of my car.

I shut the trunk and glanced at Cassie. "Ready?"

"I don't know." She bit her plump bottom lip. "It's been so long, I don't remember what I'm supposed to do." She glanced down at herself before looking back at me. "I mean, is this even the proper outfit choice for the activity?"

I gave her a once-over. She had the same tank top and cut-off shorts on that she'd been wearing earlier —the shorts that made it hard not to notice how long her tanned legs were.

Yeah, Cassie definitely had nice legs. Something I had noticed too many times when she'd cheered at the games and pep assemblies.

I swallowed. I shouldn't be thinking things like this. She was my sister's friend.

And she drove me crazy most of the time.

I forced my gaze back to her face. "What you're wearing is just fine."

"You're sure?" She had a hint of a smirk on her lips that made me think she had noticed me checking her out.

I cleared my throat and tried to act like I wasn't attracted to her. "The forecast said we'd have sunny skies all afternoon, so that should be fine. Unless, of course, you're hoping to go swimming in the lake. I know how much you enjoyed your little dip in the pool yesterday."

She made a face that told me she most definitely still harbored some hard feelings toward me for my little stunt.

"I think I'll pass on that."

I shrugged. "Then let's hit the road."

AFTER WE GOT Cassie a fishing license, we drove to Little York Lake. The afternoon sun was high in the sky, and thankfully, there weren't too many people water skiing today.

Hopefully, we'd get a few good bites from the fish.

"Are we fishing from the dock then?" Cassie asked, looking around like she was out of her element. It was strange to see her this way. Usually she was the most confident person in the room.

"Yeah, I was thinking we would just fish from here. But we can rent a boat if you'd prefer to be out on the water."

"And risk you tipping it over? No thanks."

I chuckled. "I promise you my main goal in life is not to see how many times I can dump you in a large body of water."

She held up a finger. "I look forward to allowing you to prove that to me today."

"I'll be on my best behavior."

With that settled, I sat down on the edge of the dock and indicated for her to sit beside me. And as she leaned back on her hands and let the sun warm her skin, I got to work getting our fishing poles ready.

A few minutes later, I had her fishing rod ready to go.

"Okay, so this is your pole." I handed it to her. "What you want to do is to just cast the line out several yards ahead of us."

"Cast out the line?" Her eyebrows squished

together in confusion. "How am I supposed to do that?"

"Here, let me show you."

I took the fishing pole back from her. "This is the button that you push when you want to let the line out." I demonstrated and let the baited hook drop into the water right in front of us. Then I turned the handle with my left hand and said, "When you want to bring tension back into the line, just turn this handle like so until you feel some resistance."

"So push the button to release, turn the handle to bring it back in?" she asked. "That seems simple enough."

"Yep. Not too hard." I handed her the pole. "And when you feel a tug on the line, or you just feel like recasting, all you have to do is continue winding the handle and it will come back. Easy as pie."

She nodded. Deciding that the lesson was over, I turned to get my own fishing pole ready.

I grabbed my hook out of the tackle box at my side and briefly glanced at Cassie to check on her. She was just sitting there with her feet dangling off the edge of the dock, looking at me with a sly grin on her face.

"Is something wrong?" I asked as I started tying the hook to the fishing line.

She shrugged. "Nothing's wrong."

But she kept looking at me like there was indeed something that I hadn't noticed.

Did I mess something up with the rod? It was my younger brother Caleb's rod, so it was different from mine. But I was pretty sure I'd done it right.

I gave the rod a quick once-over, but it looked fine to me. So I turned back to Cassie and asked, "Why are you looking at me like that? Are you sure nothing is wrong?"

Her grin broadened. "I was just thinking that you totally missed out on an opportunity, just barely."

I did?

What kind of opportunity? Was there a huge fish in the water that I'd missed catching with my net?

I checked the water below but didn't see a fish.

And since Cassie loved to aggravate me, of course she didn't expound any further and instead turned to look out at the lake.

She was so frustrating sometimes.

"What do you mean I missed out on an opportunity?" I asked, not able to let it go.

She slowly turned her head toward me again, her brown hair looking extra shiny in the sunlight. She lifted one shoulder. "I just meant that if you were really trying to show me what you would do on an actual date, you missed out on an opportunity to get closer right there."

"How?" I frowned.

I was pretty sure we were sitting only a few inches away from each other on the dock. What kind of an opportunity could I have missed out on?

"It doesn't matter." She waved the hand that wasn't holding her fishing pole. "You probably don't want my advice, anyway."

I bristled a little with annoyance. I didn't need her advice.

But my curiosity always did get the better of me.

I sighed and set my fishing pole on the other side of me before turning to face her.

"Okay, so since you're the expert on dating—" I gritted my teeth. "—why don't you enlighten me on what I should have done, if I was going to be the perfect date for the day?"

"Don't get your panties all in a bunch." She giggled, and I could tell she was enjoying this a little too much. "You just happened to miss out on using only the most obvious trick in the book."

"Apparently, I was never told where to buy such a book."

"Obviously," she said, digging into my ego a little bit. She sat up straighter, the improvement of her posture drawing my eyes briefly to her figure. "Any-way," she continued, and I forced my attention back to her face. "If you were really out on a date with a girl you like, you could have used your little demon-stration as an excuse to get a lot closer to her."

"So you're saying you were hoping for a more hands-on lesson?"

"Not *me,* necessarily, but as your practice date, yes. I am here to help."

"Whatever. I know you've been dying to finally get up close and personal with me." I said it more to play off the nerves that had instantly flooded my system with the prospect of having less than half a foot between us.

But I was a few years older than I'd been the last time we had to stand close together. And I had a bit more experience with girls now than I'd had back then.

I could handle this more inclusive fishing lesson without any nerves getting in the way.

So, instead of letting her think I was completely inept when it came to handling a beautiful, albeit frustrating, female, I stood on the dock and gestured for her to join me with her fishing rod.

"Let's get this hands-on lesson started."

Her eyes brightened, and I couldn't be certain,

but did she even seem excited that I was going through with this?

No. She was just excited to prove some kind of point.

I wasn't about to let that happen.

Once she was standing and had her fishing pole in hand again, I stepped closer and said, "I hope you're ready for this fishing lesson."

She gave me a flirtatious look. "Oh, I most definitely am."

"Well then," I said, moving right behind her. "Here you go."

I thought it would just be the simplest of moves— to stand behind her and guide her through the perfect cast—but I hadn't been expecting for her to smell so good or for my body to react to her the way that it did.

But as soon as I put my arms around her and guided her hands to where they needed to be on the fishing pole, my heart instantly raced in my chest.

That wasn't supposed to happen with Cassie. All those feelings for her had disappeared the night I'd declined to kiss her.

But something was most definitely happening inside my body. My skin was sparking to life in the places that were touching her, overwhelming my senses in a way they hadn't been overwhelmed in a very long time.

Since I couldn't let on that anything was happening inside of me, I cleared my throat and said, "Okay, so what you'll need to do is put your right hand right here." I helped her hands scoot up a little bit on the rod's handle. "Have your pointer finger hover right here." I carefully lifted her pointer finger to where it was supposed to go.

"Like this?" she whispered as she glanced over her shoulder at me.

Her lips were only a few inches away.

No—I pushed the thought about her lips away and focused on her eyes instead. Her brown eyes, which I had never noticed closely before, had flecks of gold mixed in with the beautiful amber color.

Stop finding reasons to think Cassie is attractive, Liam.

She's still the same girl who drove you nuts until about an hour ago.

Heat flushed my face, and I had to swallow in order to find my voice again and answer her question. "Yeah, just like that."

And of course, my voice came out shaky. What in the world? I was the quarterback of the dang football team. Not this guy who wanted to turn Cassie around in my arms and do what I had not done in that closet years ago.

"So what should I do next?" She turned her gaze back to the lake, thankfully not commenting on how weird I was acting.

I cleared my throat. "The next thing you'll want to do is pull the fishing rod backwards over your shoulder like this." I helped her with the movement, inadvertently pulling her against my chest.

I thought she'd jump away like I'd burned her or something, but when she didn't immediately put distance between us, I decided that maybe it was okay.

In fact, it kind of felt amazing to have her so close to me.

Before I could get too sidetracked by thoughts of other ways to bring her closer, I hurried to say, "And then you push the button down and bring your arm forward quickly so it releases the line and casts out into the water."

"Like this?" She did as I had instructed, and the fishing line landed in the water several yards ahead of us.

"That was perfect."

She looked over her shoulder at me with a big

smile on her face. "Thank you." Then she bit her lip, as if contemplating whether to say something.

Was she going to give me critiques of my lesson?

I already did the best I could. But had I met Cassie's high expectations?

Instead of bringing my ego down a notch, she asked, "What if a fish bites? How would I know?"

My chest loosened, relieved for some reason. "That's when you use this handle on the side of the reel and wind it slowly—"

"It would probably be appropriate for you to show me," she interrupted.

My heart stuttered in my chest. Was she saying that because of the purpose of this practice date?

Or was she wanting an excuse to stand close for longer?

Of course it's just for the lesson.

Cassie didn't see me in that way.

She never had.

But I wasn't about to pass up the opportunity to follow through, so I stepped closer and put my arms around her. I set one hand carefully on her right hip, then slid the other hand along her arm until it met her wrist. I guided her hand to the reel's handle.

I didn't know how any of this was affecting her, but I had told her in the cafe that by the end of today

I would be the only thing on her mind, so I needed to stay true to my word.

I leaned close and spoke in a low voice next to her ear. "Just turn it slowly like this," I said, helping her with the motion. "And everything will be just great."

She gasped, almost like she was pleasantly affected by my proximity. And when I let my gaze linger on her neck, I noticed it was covered with goosebumps.

She might try denying later that I had any effect on her, but that simple signal from her body told me that she liked being close to me.

8

CASSIE

IT TOOK me a few minutes to feel back to normal after Liam's quick fishing lesson. I had only suggested the hands-on lesson to tease him—to prove to him that he wasn't nearly as good with girls as he had pretended. I didn't expect to actually enjoy it.

But wow! I'd dated a lot of guys, but those short moments when Liam held me in his muscular, quarterback arms were probably the most exhilarating moments I'd had in a very long time.

I peeked sideways at Liam. He was sitting quietly beside me, contemplating the lake as he held his fishing rod.

What was he thinking about?

Had he been affected at all by our fishing lesson?

Was it bad if I hoped he was?

What was happening to me? I was supposed to hate Liam. But all I'd been doing over the past two days was notice how much more grown up he was these days. How tall he had gotten. How blue his eyes were. How his blond hair looked so touchable that my fingers itched to run their way through it.

Ugh. I must have gotten too much sun over the past two days. That would explain all these strange thoughts I was having.

Heat stroke made you crazy, right?

He must have noticed my stare because he turned his eyes on me and gave me a half-smile.

I quickly looked away, feeling my cheeks burn. And to keep myself from trying to interpret what his smile had meant, I reeled my line back in and re-cast it.

We were fishing.

Catching a fish bigger than Liam was the only goal I should have for today.

"What are you thinking about?" Liam asked, breaking the silence.

You.

"Nothing," I lied.

"Figures."

My jaw dropped and I turned to him with wide eyes. "Is that your way of saying that I have nothing going on in my brain? That it's all just silence up here unless someone is talking to me?" I touched my temple with my finger.

He held up his hands. "Whoa. Where are you getting all that from?"

"You said that it *figures* that I wasn't thinking about anything."

He shook his head and scoffed. "Despite what you think, I really don't think badly of you, Cassie." He swiveled to face me more fully. "What I meant was, it figures that you wouldn't want to share what you were actually thinking. That's the typical, Cassie thing to do. You only say what you think people want to hear."

"Yeah, right." I scowled. "I never do that with you. In fact, you're probably the one guy I never try to impress."

Okay, so maybe that wasn't all true. I *had* tried to show him how desirable I was to *other* guys.

But none of that had been for him. It was just a by-product of my true goals.

"Well, don't I feel special," he said in much too smug of a tone. "I'm the only guy who gets to know the real you."

I looked back at the water. "I let other guys get to know me."

"Prove it. We came on this practice date for you to be real and honest, instead of trying to say only what you think a guy wants to hear. So why don't you answer the question that I asked you earlier? What were you really thinking about?"

But I couldn't tell him *that!*

He didn't need a bigger ego than he already had.

Plus, it wasn't relevant anymore, anyway. He had successfully killed any good feelings that I'd had for him just barely.

"I really wasn't thinking about anything important," I said, hoping to disinterest him.

"Just try me."

I sighed and wracked my brain for something to say. I obviously couldn't tell him that I thought he looked like a Greek god, but I could say something that I'd been thinking about earlier.

"Fine, if you must know. I was thinking about going fishing with my bio dad when I was younger."

"Your bio dad?" Liam's demeanor instantly went from lighthearted to somber.

I nodded. "Yeah. We lived with him until I was seven."

"You did?" He squinted his eyes in the sunlight as he studied my face. "Y-you've never talked about him before."

I wound the handle of my reel around a few times as I tried to decide how to continue. Liam had told me he wanted to get to know the real me. Maybe now was the time to open up about something that I didn't like to talk about.

So I drew in a deep breath and gazed out at the water. It was easier to talk when I wasn't looking at anyone.

"I know that I've always just told everyone in Ridgewater that I didn't have a dad before Isaac, but that's not exactly true."

"I figured it wasn't," he said. "Immaculate conception doesn't seem to happen much these days."

I laughed, grateful for the ease in the tension for a moment. But I still didn't look at him. *Couldn't* look at him because I didn't want to see whatever expression he had on his face when I finished talking about the man who had been in my life long enough for me to think he'd be around forever, before he decided to dump me like an unwanted leech.

Liam cleared his throat, breaking the silence. "So you said you were thinking about how you went fishing with your dad when you were younger?"

"Yeah." I nodded. "Usually we just shot hoops together on the weekends, but there were a couple of weekends that he brought me to the lake."

"So what happened to him?"

A lot had happened.

And yet, really not that much.

"Basically, he moved to Canada and pretty much forgot he had a family here in Ridgewater?"

"He's in Canada?" Surprise showed on his face. "For some reason I always assumed he must have died or gone to jail or something."

He might as well have. He would have had as much presence in my life that way as he did, anyway.

"No, he's still alive and well in Canada. At least, that's what my grandma tells me."

Liam frowned. "So what happened?"

"There's a reason why I don't like to talk about it." I adjusted my position on the dock, pulling my shorts down a little lower on my legs to protect more skin from the sun. "It's kind of embarrassing."

Liam put his hand on my leg. My skin warmed where he touched me.

"You don't have to tell me if you don't want to." His eyes were sincere. "I know I said this practice date was for you to practice being more open about who you are, but you don't have to tell me if you don't want to."

My heart softened at his words. He was giving

me a way out. He wasn't going to pressure me into telling my story.

But there was something in that small offering that made me actually want to tell him.

I wanted to tell someone about what had really happened to make me call my first dad "my sperm donor" instead of *Dad* when I talked about him.

"No, it's okay. I can talk about it." At least, I would try to. I mean, it happened a long time ago. I shouldn't let what he had done affect me so much anymore. He didn't deserve to have any sort of influence in my life.

"Did something happen after he moved to Canada?" Liam asked, reminding me of where I'd left off in my story.

"Yeah." I nodded. "So like I said, my dad got a job in Canada when I was seven. He had been out of work for about six months, I guess, so he was just desperate to get a job. My mom was teaching elementary at the time and wanted to finish the school year with her students, so they decided that my dad would go on ahead of us and my mom and I would join him a few months later once the school year had ended."

"That sounds like a reasonable plan."

"Yeah, you'd think so," I said, remembering back

to that time. "Anyway, as the end of the school year approached, my mom and I started packing everything up in our apartment. She told the school district she wouldn't be coming back the next year and they found a teacher to teach her class the next year.

"We only had a few weeks to go before we would be moving and we were getting excited to be with my dad again after being separated for several months." I paused, not sure of how to say the next thing. But deciding that the straightforward approach was probably best, I said, "That's when things went down the toilet. My mom always called my dad at night to catch up on their days, but one night someone else answered his phone."

"No..." Liam gasped, his eyes growing wider.

"Yes." I tucked some stray hair behind my ear. "Apparently, there was a single mom with three kids who lived in the same building as my dad, and they ended up spending too much time together."

"So what happened next?"

"Well, after my mom went all berserk on him, they tried to work things out. But the damage had been done, so we never ended up moving to Canada. He and that lady, Felisha, got married a few weeks after the divorce was finalized, and I didn't even get invited to the wedding."

"What?" Liam raised his voice.

"And that's not even the worst part of the whole story."

"It gets worse?" He gave me a look that told me he didn't understand how it could get any worse than it already was.

I looked at my feet dangling over the edge of the dock. "Things seemed to be okay for the first two years after the divorce. I would go visit my dad and Felisha for a couple of weeks in the summer. But then I guess it just got too expensive for my dad to fly me out there or something because he stopped trying to see me."

"Was this before or after you moved to Ridgewater?"

"It was before."

He nodded.

"Anyway, I only talked to my dad on the phone a couple of times a month after that. My mom got a new job in Ridgewater so we moved here and just tried to start over. I kept playing basketball, hoping that my dad might come to one of my games, since that had always been our thing together. But then, out of the blue, my mom got a call from my dad, asking her if she could petition the court for them to take away his parental rights. She and Isaac had been married for a while, and I guess my dad and Felisha saw that as the perfect chance for my dad to get out of paying the child support he had never actually paid."

"He wanted to give up his parental rights?"

"Yup."

"So did Isaac adopt you then?"

"Yeah. My mom decided to let my bio dad off the hook since he wasn't doing anything for me, anyway, and Isaac was happy to legally take the spot he'd already been filling for the past few years."

"When did all of this happen?"

"It was in eighth grade."

We were quiet for a little while until he suddenly twisted toward me. "Wait, was that around the time you decided to quit playing basketball and do cheerleading instead?"

I was surprised he'd put two and two together.

"That's exactly why I made the switch. I wanted to get rid of any reminders I had of the guy who decided I wasn't important enough to be in his life anymore."

"I had no idea."

"Yeah, I don't really like telling people that I was

rejected by the one guy who was supposed to love me no matter what."

Which was precisely why I was careful not to let other guys get close enough that they could hurt me. I had to be smarter with how connected I let myself get to people. I had to protect myself from ever getting hurt like that again.

"I'm sorry about your bio dad. Sounds like a real piece of work."

"Yeah. It's weird. I mean, he was a really good dad for the first seven years of my life. Then it's like something changed in his brain when he moved away. He became a different person."

I stopped, not sure I wanted to admit to the next part. But since this seemed to be my "bare your whole soul to Liam session," I decided that I might as well just tell it all.

"For a while, I actually thought something must have been wrong with me. I wondered if maybe after my dad had been around Felisha's kids, he realized that they were more of the children that he'd always wanted. They were always so well behaved while I'd been pretty crazy. I couldn't hold still and was always running around being busy. They, on the other hand, could sit for hours and just read books."

"Hey." Liam touched my leg again. "Don't think

that. There's nothing wrong with you, Cassie. It's not your fault that he messed up royally and gave up the opportunity to be with you."

I looked down, feeling tears prick at the back of my eyes.

Liam scooted closer, setting his fishing pole down on the other side of him. He took my face in his hands. "He's the one who's missing out. I know tons of guys who are just tripping over themselves because they want you to notice them."

"I know." I wiped at the tear that was beginning to leak out of the corner of my eye.

He smiled. "You know?"

I let out a quick laugh, despite feeling like I was going to cry. "I don't have all those ex-boyfriends for nothing."

Another tear escaped, but Liam wiped it away with his thumb.

"You deserve a guy who will cherish you. Someone you can let know all the different parts of you and who knows how lucky he is to be with you."

My heart thrummed to life, beating so fast it could give a hummingbird a run for its money.

Liam's gaze dipped down to my lips and my stomach twisted.

Was he going to kiss me?

Did I want him to kiss me?

I glanced at his soft, pink lips. I'd been presented with the opportunity to kiss him three and a half years ago, but nothing had come from it. And it was probably crazy, but I didn't want to miss out on this chance to see what it was like to kiss Liam Turner.

I lifted my gaze to his eyes again. They had changed in the past few seconds. And they were looking at me in a way that made it hard to breathe.

"Cassie?" He spoke my name like a caress. "Is it okay if I..."

But before he could finish the thought, I felt a tug on the fishing rod that I'd all but forgotten.

"Aah!" I yelped as I fumbled to get a better hold on the handle, but before I could get a good grip, it was yanked out of my hand.

It landed in the water with a quiet splash and quickly began to sink.

And I could only blame what I did next on a moment of insanity, because I jumped in the water to get it.

"YOU KNOW you didn't have to jump in the water to get the fishing pole," I said to Cassie as I reached down to give her a hand and help her out of the lake.

Did she freak out at the prospect of me kissing her? Did she intentionally throw her fishing pole in the water as an excuse to jump in the lake to get away from me?

I still couldn't believe that I'd almost kissed her.

I'd almost kissed the girl who had driven me bonkers for the past several years. The girl who was also my sister's best friend who happened to be staying at my house for the next few days.

What was I thinking?

I couldn't kiss Cassie.

Sure, she was gorgeous, and we'd actually gotten

along really well today. But that was just one day. You couldn't go from detesting a person one day to wanting to ask her to be your girlfriend the next.

At least, sane people didn't do things like that.

But the past twenty hours had me seriously questioning my sanity. Because I had a serious case of Cassie on the brain.

"I didn't want to lose your brother's fishing rod." She handed me the rod first then put her hand in mine so I could pull her up and out of the water.

When she got to her feet, her clothes clung to her body and dripped water onto the dock.

"Thanks for helping me." She pulled the fabric of her shirt away from her body, which helped me to bring my eyes back up to her face.

"No problem," I said, my voice sounding more froggy than usual. I knew I needed to focus on something other than the fact that Cassie's drenched shirt left little to the imagination, so I hurried to say, "For a girl who didn't want to get in the pool yesterday, you certainly jumped into the lake fast."

She wrung the water out of her ponytail. "Yeah, well. I guess getting thrown in yesterday helped to change my mind about large bodies of water."

I grinned, and just because I couldn't help but

tease her, I said, "But there's no chlorine in the lake. And fish poop in it all day..."

Her eyes went wide, and her body went rigid. "Why did you have to remind me of that, Liam?" She shook, like she was imagining all sorts of parasites crawling all over her now wet body.

"Sorry." I laughed, crossing my arms in front of me because she looked so annoyed that she might just hit me. "How about we get you back to my house so you can shower the lake off before the party tonight?"

"Yes, please." She sighed. "I'd rather not look like a drowned kitten when I'm talking to Luke."

Luke.

His name suddenly grated on my nerves more than it ever had before.

I liked the guy enough. He was a great linebacker and cool to hang out with. But the idea of Cassie and Luke dating bothered me more than it had yesterday.

Would she tell Luke about her bio dad like she'd told me? Would she take my advice and finally get a boyfriend who'll stick around for longer than a few weeks because he actually got to know her this time around?

Or would she try to jump in a lake if he tried to kiss her tonight?

I could hope, right?

But Luke was one of the most popular guys in our grade. If he'd healed from his mom's passing enough to date again, there was no way Cassie wouldn't sink her teeth into him.

I decided that it wouldn't do any good for me to stew and wonder about the what-ifs, so I started packing up the fishing gear so we could get out of here.

I'd find out what happened between her and Luke Davenport soon enough.

———

WE WERE ALMOST to my car when Cassie suddenly grabbed my arm and stopped in her tracks.

"What?" I asked, turning to see why she'd stopped us.

"Can we just wait a minute?"

I furrowed my brow. "Why?"

She pointed toward the parking lot. "Because Jess Brooks is coming our way. I can't have him thinking that I've gone downhill since our breakup. I mean, would you want to see an ex when you look like I do right now?"

I followed to where she was pointing and saw

Jess Brooks shutting the trunk of his lime green Camaro. He was carrying a quilt and what looked like a chocolate shake in one hand.

"Is that his new girlfriend?" I asked when I saw a short brunette with olive-complected skin step up beside him.

Cassie shook her head. "No, that's just his best friend, Eliana. Though, they should probably start dating. His inability to put girlfriends above his best friend is one of the main reasons why we broke up."

I watched the two as they headed toward the park that was right next to the lake. They did look like they could be a couple from how closely they were walking beside each other.

But they weren't holding hands or anything, so most likely it was strictly platonic.

I knew that if I was dating Cassie, I wouldn't be able to keep myself from taking her hand in mine any chance I got.

My heart stuttered to a stop when I realized where my train of thought had just led me.

Had I seriously just thought about *dating* Cassie?

I glanced at her, my eyes catching onto where she still clung to my arm. It definitely didn't feel unpleasant to have her standing so close to me.

"Hide me," Cassie suddenly said before stepping directly behind me.

I scanned the perimeter to see that Jess had looked briefly in our direction.

"You really don't want Jess to see you with me, do you?" I asked.

"You already know that's not it." Her voice was muffled because she was standing so close to my back in her attempt to disappear from sight. "If I looked half decent right now, the first thing I'd do was parade you around in front of him just so Jess would think that I'd moved on."

"You would?"

The thought warmed my insides.

"Of course!"

"So you're not embarrassed to be seen with me?"

I heard her sigh. "No, Liam. I'm not embarrassed to be with you. I'm embarrassed to be with me."

I chuckled and turned around so I could see her. "You really don't look all that bad right now, Cassie. Sure you're a little damp right now—" I flipped her damp ponytail with my hand. "—but it hasn't stopped me from checking you out."

She raised her eyebrows, her jaw dropping. "You've been checking me out?"

My neck prickled with heat. Yeah, I probably shouldn't have said that out loud.

But since it was out in the open, I said, "I am a guy, you know. And yeah, sure, if pressed I may say that you're attractive."

"Even after falling in the lake?" She looked up at me sweetly.

"*Falling* in the lake?" I teased.

"Okay, fine. Even after jumping into the lake?"

"Yes. Even after jumping into the lake." I smiled and turned so we were side by side again, putting my arm around her shoulder. "Now let's get you out of here before Jess can see what he's missing out on and try to win you back."

10

CASSIE

WE MADE it back to Liam's house around six. I had dried most of the way on the drive home, but I couldn't get the image of fish poop particles sitting on my skin out of my mind, so I took a shower before coming down to dinner with the Turner family.

"We left some tortellini for you on a plate," Mrs. Turner said to me as she put the dishes in the dishwasher. "It should still be warm."

I thanked her for thinking of me and quickly ate my dinner. Raven would be over soon to get ready for tonight's party with Alyssa and me, and since I had to completely re-do my hair and makeup in the next hour and a half, I didn't have much time to spare on eating.

I looked around the living area, curious to see where Liam had gone after dinner. But he wasn't anywhere in sight. He was probably hanging out in his room, figuring out what he was going to say to Bridgett tonight.

An unexpected pang hurt my chest at the idea of Liam talking to Bridgett.

Was it so much to hope that she and Ryan were going to try doing the long-distance relationship thing? New York City was only four hours away. They could still meet up a couple of weekends a month.

It was that train of thought that made me realize something.

I was jealous of Bridgett.

Jealous of any girl Liam might be interested in dating.

Which told me one thing.

I liked Liam.

And I wanted him to like me back.

I dug my fork into my dinner and focused on eating. I didn't need to think about Liam taking another girl fishing at the lake. I didn't need to think about him putting his arms around her as he gave her a hands-on lesson like he'd given me today.

I didn't need to think about him kissing anyone.

I covered my heart with my hand. Why did the thought of him kissing another girl hurt? It wouldn't have bothered me two days ago.

I wasn't supposed to fall for him.

But I think that I had.

11

LIAM

I SHOWERED and put on my favorite V-neck T-shirt and jeans after dinner. The one time Cassie had complimented my choice of clothes, I'd been wearing this exact outfit.

Was it bad that I hoped she'd notice me wearing it again tonight?

I knew I was supposed to be thinking about what Bridgett might think of me, since, according to Cassie, our practice date today had been all about me trying to catch her interest.

But as I did my hair and sprayed myself with a small spritz of cologne, the thoughts that ran through my mind were about whether Cassie would like this scent or not. I didn't care what anyone else thought of me tonight.

After brushing my teeth and using mouthwash, I went upstairs to wait for the girls to finish getting ready.

I could hear their giggling voices from Alyssa's bedroom as I made my way into the living room. They were probably all laughing and talking about how Cassie was going to land her next boyfriend tonight.

To drown out the noise, I turned on the TV to find a sports channel to watch.

The sun had sunk a little lower in the sky by the time Raven and Alyssa came into the living room. Cassie must be finishing up the final touches of her look tonight.

"We're ready," Alyssa said, grabbing a light sweater from the entryway closet. "Trey says he's just going to meet me there, so he can probably just give us all a ride home afterwards and you can hang out with your buddies."

"Sounds good." I turned off the TV and stood from the couch, pulling my keys out of my jeans pocket. "Let's get on the road then."

Alyssa and Raven turned to head out the door. I was about to follow them outside when Cassie walked into the living room.

I swallowed when I saw her.

She looked good.

No, she looked *gorgeous*.

Her long brown hair framed her face in soft shiny curls. She'd re-done her makeup, giving herself a dramatic yet not-overdone look. And the light pink blouse and white lacy shorts she wore looked amazing on her petite figure.

She wasn't that tall, but that girl had legs that went on for days.

I blinked my eyes shut before she could catch my glassy-eyed stare.

"Hi, Liam," she said. Her voice sounded more timid than usual. "Are Alyssa and Raven already outside?"

I nodded, momentarily speechless.

Why was I taking her to this party again?

Why wasn't I begging her to stay here with me instead?

I pushed those thoughts away. If she didn't want me, she didn't want me.

It wasn't like I hadn't seen her date guys before.

Was it bad to hope that if she and Luke did end up dating after this, it would last as long as her other relationships? Over in a week or two so there was a chance for me to win her over.

But would she ever forgive me for all the teasing I'd done to her in the past?

Probably not.

I should have realized sooner that I liked her, so I could have behaved better.

When I realized that she was looking at me like I was missing a screw in my head—probably because I was just silently studying her—I gestured to the front door and said, "After you."

Alyssa and Raven were already in the backseat of my car when we got there, leaving the passenger seat open for Cassie.

We climbed onto our respective sides. I buckled myself in and reached for the gear shift between our seats. At the same time, Cassie was stretching out her seatbelt in front of her and our fingers brushed against each other accidentally.

"Sorry," she whispered.

My fingers sparked to life where they'd been touched by her. I flexed my hand at the feeling and said, "It's okay."

I waited for her to buckle in her seatbelt before trying to shift my car into drive, though all I wanted was to take her hand in mine and hold it.

But I pushed those thoughts away and pulled onto the road instead. And to keep my mind from trying to figure out ways to convince Cassie to go get ice cream at Emrie's Ice Cream Shop instead of going to the party, I focused on what Alyssa and Raven were talking about in the back.

"Maybe Liam will know. He's on the football team with him," I heard Raven say once I'd tuned in into their conversation.

"Who?" I asked. "Are you talking about Luke?"

"No." I saw Raven shake her head in the rearview mirror. "We were talking about Noah Taylor. We heard that he and Ashlyn broke up, and I'm hoping he comes to the party so I can cheer him up a little."

I'd bet she wanted to "cheer him up," all right. She wasn't nicknamed Rebound Raven for nothing.

"So did he say anything at football practice about coming to the party?" Raven asked.

"Not that I remember."

He was a great football player. He certainly knew how to hit hard. But he never really talked to me about his life outside of football. And with how he showed up to practice with new bruises or cuts each week, I wondered if he didn't talk about what was going on in his life for a reason.

"Well, hopefully he's there. I need to get on his radar before school starts next week."

The girls continued chatting about who else they

were hoping to run into at the party, and I did my best to act normal when I heard Cassie mention a couple names of other guys.

She gets in and out of relationships all the time. I told myself. *It's not the end of the world if she finds someone interesting tonight.*

Maybe if I kept telling myself that enough times, I might actually believe it.

12

CASSIE

"YOU WERE quiet on the drive over here. Is something wrong?" I asked Liam after Raven and Alyssa left us in the parking lot so they could check out the party.

"I was just thinking about stuff," he said, his face more solemn than usual.

What had happened? He'd been in a pretty good mood all day when we'd been together. Had something changed?

"What kinds of things are you thinking of?" I pried. Admittedly, I had been pretty quiet too, just letting Alyssa and Raven fill the air space as I took surreptitious glances at Liam and wondered what he was thinking about.

Was he quiet for the same reasons I was?

He'd given me a different sort of look when I'd walked into his family's living room earlier. My heart had gone into overload as he'd studied me, and I had been sure that he had watched me with admiration in his eyes.

But I could have been wrong. I'd been wrong about guys a lot.

"I wasn't thinking about anything important." He glanced at the clearing in the trees where the bonfire was already burning with kids from school standing around it. "We should probably get you to the party. Luke is probably waiting for you."

My stomach twisted.

But what if I didn't want to talk to Luke anymore? What if I just wanted to stay with Liam?

"Are you anxious to get to Bridgett then?" I asked, not really wanting to hear his answer.

In my dream world, he'd take my hand and we'd leave this party right now. We'd maybe go back to the dock and I would try to get him to kiss me like I'd thought he might do earlier before I jumped into the lake.

I should have just let the dang fishing pole sink into the water.

Maybe then he wouldn't be pushing me to talk to

Luke and he wouldn't be looking forward to talking to Bridgett.

He pushed his hands into his pockets. "I supposed talking to Bridgett was what you prepared me for with our practice date, huh?" He kicked a rock.

He said, "you prepared me for," and not "that he was excited to do."

Did that mean that he had possibly changed his mind about Bridgett? I was about to ask him when Alyssa and Raven came back through the trees.

"What's the hold up, guys?" Alyssa said, looking out of breath, like she and Raven had been in a hurry to find us again. "Raven and I just spotted Luke finishing up his British guy impersonation for Jake and Kellen. Now's your chance to talk to him."

I cast Liam a hesitant glance.

He just looked at me with those deep blue eyes of his, his jaw flexing. Was he upset that my friends were whisking me away from him?

"I don't know..." I told my friends, feeling a war wage in my brain. *Would I look stupid if I tried to stay with Liam?*

Was I just imagining he might like me back just because I wanted it so bad?

But I didn't get a chance to finish my thought.

Alyssa and Raven both flanked me, and then Raven said, "Since when do you of all people get nervous over talking to a guy? Let's go."

And with that, I was walking toward Luke, when all I wanted to do was stay with Liam.

13

LIAM

"WHY ARE you in such a bad mood?" Alyssa asked after we'd been at the party for about thirty minutes.

I was sitting on one of the logs around the fire pit with her, trying not to think about what Luke and Cassie might be talking about right now. If I was sticking to the plan Cassie and I had come up with earlier today, I would have been looking for Bridgett or even some other girl to practice my "new girl-charming skills" on. But I just didn't care about any of that right now.

There was only one girl I wanted to charm, and she was currently talking to Luke Davenport somewhere in the woods.

"Liam..." Alyssa prodded when I didn't answer her.

I sighed. "I'm just tired." I looked at her. "Once Trey shows up to give you girls your ride home, I'll probably head out."

My sister studied me for a moment. "Are you sure nothing's wrong?"

"Yep. I'm just great." I hunched over, setting my forearms on my knees. I just gazed into the fire, watching the flames lick the wood and disappear into the night sky.

"You certainly don't look great."

"Gee, thanks, sis."

She let out an exasperated sigh. "You know what I mean."

"It's just been a long day," I said, hoping to get her off my back.

Alyssa bent over on her knees to get on my eye level. "Cassie told me you guys hung out. Did she tire you out today?"

"No..."

"So what did you two do together?"

"She didn't tell you?"

I'd guess I should be grateful Cassie hadn't told Raven and Alyssa all about how she had to jump into the lake to get away from my attempt at kissing her.

She shrugged. "I forgot to ask. I was too busy telling her what I did with Trey this afternoon."

Alyssa frowned. "Did you guys just fight all after-noon like you usually do?"

"No." I picked up a piece of bark off the ground and tossed it into the fire. "It was actually the opposite."

"You guys got along?" Alyssa raised her eyebrows. "That has to be a first."

"It was actually nice."

"Wait." Her jaw dropped. "Did you just say that spending the afternoon with Cassie was *nice?*"

"Yeah." I let my voice drift off as I remembered our lunch and fishing trip. We'd had great conversation with some fun bantering back and forth. Then she'd opened up to me about her bio dad.

That had to have meant something to her, right?

But it had been a *practice* date, not a real one. Cassie was just a really great actress, it looked like. Well, I'd guess that would serve her well when she tries out for the spring play.

I could feel Alyssa studying me for a long moment, making me uncomfortable. Would she be able to tell that I liked her friend?

"Do I have something on my face?" I asked after a moment, hoping to draw my sister's attention away from whatever she was thinking about me and Cassie.

"No," she said. "But I do wonder..."

I composed the expression on my face as smoothly as I could. "What do you wonder?"

"I wonder if maybe you might have feelings for Cassie."

My face must have given me away because Alyssa gasped.

"You like Cassie?" she whispered, her eyes bright with excitement.

And I really must have been in a weird mood tonight, because instead of denying it, I simply lifted a shoulder and said, "Maybe."

She sat up straight. "Then what the heck are you doing here moping around instead of talking to her?"

I sat up, too, and sighed. "She wanted to talk to Luke."

"So?"

I ran a hand through my hair. "How can I compete with Luke? He's a great guy."

"And so are you."

I waved the thought away. "Until today, Cassie and I could barely stand to be in the same room as each other. She doesn't like me in that way. She barely likes me at all."

"Give yourself some credit, Liam. I saw her

checking you out when we were at the pool yesterday. She's definitely attracted to you."

Cassie had checked me out?

"You did?"

"Yes. And when you were mowing the lawn as
well, now that I think of it."

"Really?"

"Yes, really."

I was about to get my hopes up when I realized
that just because someone thought you were attractive, didn't mean they wanted to go on a date
with you.

Not a real date, anyway.

Alyssa must have sensed my doubts because she
said, "It's worth a shot. I mean, what's the worse that
could happen?"

"She could jump into the lake again."

"She could what?"

I explained to her all about what had happened
at the lake earlier today.

"Maybe she was just surprised."

"Or maybe she wasn't."

Alyssa held up her hands. "Fine. You don't need
to go after what you want. It doesn't matter to me
either way, really."

I was just about to tell Alyssa that it didn't matter

to me, either, when Luke suddenly appeared in the clearing. He was striding quickly away from the spot he and Cassie had gone in to talk. And from the look on his face, he didn't look happy.

What had happened?

Was Cassie okay?

A second later, Cassie appeared in the clearing, her gaze following after Luke as he walked toward the parking lot.

When he climbed into his Jeep a moment later, she turned around, shoulders slumped, and went back into the trees.

"What do you think happened?" I asked Alyssa who was watching the same scene as I was.

"I have no idea," she said. "Maybe I should go check on her."

She made ready to stand, but I put my hand on her shoulder. "No, I'll go check on her."

Alyssa nodded, a faint smile finding its way onto her lips. "Yes, go be her knight in shining armor."

The idea of me being any girl's knight in shining armor was laughable, but I didn't feel like wasting time to argue the point with my sister. Instead, I headed toward Cassie.

14

CASSIE

"CASSIE?"

I startled when I heard my name spoken by a deep voice. The owner of the voice stepped closer, and when I saw who it was, I wanted to run away.

It was Liam.

I didn't want him to see me like this.

I turned away, shielding my face from his view so he wouldn't see the fresh tears on my cheeks.

"Cassie?" he said again, this time only a couple of feet away. "Are you okay?"

"I'm fine." I wiped at my cheek before turning back toward him with a smile plastered to my face.

He stopped his approach and narrowed his eyes as he studied me. The sun had mostly dipped behind the horizon by now, so I hoped he wouldn't be able to see the moisture in my eyes.

"Did something happen with Luke?"

That depended on what his definition of something was. *Something* had most definitely happened to cause Luke to bolt right when I was in the middle of telling him a funny story—but as to what exactly had caused him to do that was lost on me.

When I didn't answer, Liam stepped in front of me, took my shoulders in his hands, and made me face him. "Did Luke do something to you?"

"No." I shook my head. "He didn't do anything."

"Then what's wrong? Why did he just drive off?" His expression softened and he wiped at a tear on my cheek with his thumb. "And why does it look like you've been crying?"

I looked down, feeling stupid.

"I really don't know what happened. One moment I was telling him about this funny thing my mom did last week, and the next thing I know, he's standing up and running away like his pants got lit on fire."

Liam closed his eyes briefly and sighed before opening them again. "I think I know what went wrong."

I furrowed my brow. "You do?"

How in the world could Liam know just from that little bit of information?

Liam nodded and let his hands drop from my shoulders. "I think it was the story about your mom."

"What?"

Luke liked to do impersonations from movies to make his friends laugh. I thought for sure he would like to hear a funny story himself.

Did he want to be the only funny person at the party tonight?

"I think it was the story about your mom. You see..." Liam bit his lip, like he was hesitant to tell me whatever he had to say. "You see, Luke's mom just passed away in July."

"She did?" Dread filled me when I realized just how hard it probably was for Luke to laugh about moms right now.

"Yeah. She had cancer for a long time, and it finally won."

"How did I not know about this?"

"I don't think very many people know yet."

I nodded, but then realizing something more, I asked, "Why didn't you tell me? Did you want me to make a fool of myself tonight or something?"

"No." He shook his head. "It wasn't that at all."

"Then what was it?"

"I didn't think it was my story to tell. Luke hasn't really been talking about it with anyone. I only found out because I shared a room with him at football camp."

"Still, you could have at least warned me."

"I know. I'm sorry. If I'm being honest, my head was kind of in a weird spot all day and I didn't think to tell you tonight."

Could he have been thinking the same things as I was? Had he been as distracted by whatever was happening between us as I had been?

"Why was your head in a weird spot?"

He stared at a tree a few feet away from us and sighed. Then, after a long moment, he faced me again. It was hard to make out his features in the dim lighting, but what I could see was an intensity in his eyes that hadn't been there before.

And was there a hint of desire?

My stomach muscles tightened at the thought. Never before in my life had I wanted someone to desire me so much.

He took a step closer, taking my hand in his. "I was in a weird place this afternoon because—"

A twig snapped behind me. Followed by some giggling from a female voice, and then a shhhing sound from a deeper voice.

An instant later, a guy and a girl from our school walked through the trees a few feet away. They looked around them, like they were hiding from someone. Then the guy leaned against a tree and pulled the girl with grayish-blonde hair against him, and they started kissing.

I glanced back at Liam, who was studying the couple.

Well, this was awkward now, wasn't it?

I looked down and noticed that Liam was still holding my hand.

What was he about to say?

Why was he in a weird mood?

He turned his gaze away from the couple with the corner of his mouth tilted up in amusement. "Is that Easton Stevens with someone?"

I narrowed my eyes. It was hard to tell in the dim light.

The couple separated for a moment, like they were trying to catch their breath, and I was able to see the guy's face a little better.

Indeed, it was Easton Stevens, Noah Taylor's best friend, who was kissing some girl. Easton and his sister Lexi were famous at Ridgewater High for having purity rings and a vow to keep themselves sex free until they were at least in college, since their older sister had become a teenage mom and their dad was paranoid it would happen again.

I'd never seen Eason date very much, so it was shocking to see him sneaking around with the light-haired girl.

They started kissing again, and when Easton pushed his hands into the girl's hair, making it so I could see her profile better, I recognized her immediately.

I gasped. "That's Juliette Cardini!"

"It is?" Liam looked back at the couple, leaning his head forward to get a better view.

"Yeah, I'm pretty sure," I said.

And now that I had seen more of her face, I totally recognized the skirt she was wearing.

Liam scrunched up his face like he was baffled. "What the heck are those two doing sneaking around? Isn't she his little sister's best friend?"

"Yeah. I'm pretty sure she is."

We were quiet for a moment, both of us so stunned by the couple that we couldn't seem to look away.

As Juliette fisted her hands in Easton's brown hair, I couldn't help but wonder what it would be like to kiss my own friend's older brother.

My heart raced with the thought.

But then I remembered the way Liam had seemed so surprised that those two would be together at all, because of Easton's sister.

Did that mean he thought the idea of anyone dating his sister's friend was somehow wrong?

My heart sank. If that was true, then he probably hadn't been thinking any romantic thoughts about me earlier after all.

Maybe I'd just totally imagined that almost-kiss at the lake.

As my disappointment washed over me, I must have sighed too loudly because Liam turned to me again and whispered, "Is something wrong?"

I bit my lip, considering bringing up a completely random subject.

But no. On our practice date today, he'd told me that guys wanted me to be more authentic. To say what I actually wanted to say.

So I was going to finally do just that.

I took a deep breath and looked up at Liam's handsome face. "Do you think it's weird that Easton would be sneaking around with his sister's best friend?"

Liam's eyes studied me for a long moment, like he was trying to gauge how I would react to whatever his answer was. He pressed his lips together and looked down to where he was still holding my hand in his.

He ran his thumb across my knuckles, causing my nerve endings to spark to life.

"If you would have asked me that question a day ago, I would have told you that yes, a guy dating his sister's best friend would be weird."

He stopped, and my face flashed with heat, my heart banging so hard in my chest it felt like I was on the verge of a heart attack.

"But..." Liam continued, making my heart beat even more erratically.

"But what?" I asked, my voice coming out just barely above a whisper.

"But something changed today." The fingers of his free hand brushed some stray hairs behind my ear, causing my skin to tingle everywhere he touched. "And since there is no lake for you to jump into right now, I'm going to go out on a scary limb here and say that, after today at the lake, I'm starting to think that dating my own sister's friend is exactly what I want to do."

I swallowed, feeling like I might faint from relief and happiness as my heart soared in my chest. "Are you talking about me?"

He nodded. "Yes."

And before I could think or react or do anything, Liam was slipping his hand into the hair at the nape of my neck and tilting my face toward him and kissing me. His lips were soft and slow, and I may have teased him earlier about not knowing how to get a girl to go on a second date with him, but I had never been more wrong about something in my life.

"Promise you're not considering jumping into a lake right now?" he asked, his breathing slightly ragged.

"Of course not," I gasped. In fact, if he didn't kiss me again, I would totally hold it against him forever.

He must have sensed how much I wanted him to kiss me again, because a second later, he was pulling me into his arms, pressing his lips into mine again, and giving me a long, slow, and deep kiss that made it hard to think. Hard to breathe.

I was seriously at risk of fainting from lack of oxygen because I didn't want to take the time to breathe. I just wanted his lips on mine. Like I was dehydrated in the desert and he was the last drop of water around.

"I think I was wrong about your dating skills," I mumbled against his lips after a moment.

"You were?" he asked, breathlessly.

I nodded, pushing my hand into his hair and tangling my fingers into it. "I was very wrong."

His lips quirked up into that half-smile I loved so much, and he pulled me close to him again.

His mouth weaved a spell over my mind, and his hands moved in slow circles along my back—pressing our bodies so close together that there was no space left between us.

It was then that I realized that Liam had probably known all along that he was a master in the kissing arena. He'd known that he needed to use his skills sparingly, so he didn't overwhelm the female population at Ridgewater High so much.

No other guys would have had a chance against our smart, breathtakingly handsome quarterback if he'd let on to just how good he was.

Because if anyone knew what it was like to kiss Liam Turner, they'd forget about everything.

I was certainly having a hard time remembering why I'd ever been interested in anyone but him.

I let my other hand slip up his ribcage until it rested just over his heart. His years of football and lifting weights had done great things for his physique. He was no longer the lanky guy I'd been stuck in a closet with all those years ago. He was more like a man. A strong man who knew his strength enough that he didn't have to brag about it.

But even though his muscular chest felt so nice under the palm of my hand, the thing I noticed most was how fast his heart was beating.

It was racing just as fast as mine.

He was enjoying this closeness, too.

He pulled away for a moment, as if catching his breath. He leaned his forehead against mine, his gaze penetrating and more vulnerable than I'd expected.

Running his thumb across my bottom lip, he whispered, "I should have kissed you years ago."

My stomach twisted with pleasure at his words.

"At the Carmichaels' end-of-summer party?"

He swallowed, his Adam's apple bobbing with the movement. "Yes."

"But didn't you say it would be like kissing your sister?" I asked, remembering that day.

"I did." He nodded, his gaze darting back and forth between my eyes. "But even though I said it, it couldn't have been further from the truth."

What?

"I liked you back then, Cassie." He pushed away the hair that had fallen into my eyes, tucking it behind my ear. "I was just nervous and had no idea what I was doing. So I made the stupid comment."

"You liked me?"

I shook my head. It didn't make any sense. I thought he'd been disgusted by me.

He must have sensed how confused I was by this, because he took my face in his hands and said, "I know it doesn't make sense that I would do that, but it's true. I had a huge crush on you all through my freshman year."

My whole body flooded with heat.

But before I could form an intelligent response, he said, "Though if we're really being honest here, that tiny crush has nothing on what I'm feeling for you right now."

A huge smile spread across my face. "Oh really?"

He smiled wickedly back at me. "Yes, but instead of telling you all about it, how about I just show you?"

And in the next instant, he was gathering me up in his arms again and kissing me.

15

LIAM

"WE SHOULD PROBABLY GO INSIDE NOW, huh?" I asked Cassie after we'd sat in my car outside my house for the past hour, just talking and laughing, and yes, kissing.

She ran her thumb across mine, our hands intertwined on her lap. "I don't want to say goodnight, though. Today has just been too perfect."

"It has been perfect." I smiled at her, taking in her peaceful expression in the moonlight. "But we still have a few days left of summer to spend together."

"True," she allowed. "But do you think your parents are going to be okay with me staying at your house for the next few days? Knowing that we're suddenly boyfriend and girlfriend is probably going to make them nervous."

I smiled at her use of *boyfriend* and *girlfriend*. I'd never had an official girlfriend before. But I really liked the idea of Cassie being my girlfriend. There was just something so right about it.

"They'll probably be more confused than nervous," I said.

She smiled and leaned her head against her headrest. "I guess I can understand that."

"But really, you're only at our house for, like, four more days. They'll probably just put Alyssa on high alert while they're at work, and then put a lock on my door at night, so you don't try any more attempts at revenge."

"Dang it." She snapped her fingers. "I still need to get you back for throwing me in the pool."

"I'm pretty sure that watching you walk off to talk with Luke tonight was torture enough."

Cassie gave me a gentle look that made my heart turn to mush. She leaned over the armrest. "Fine then. As long as you let me kiss you whenever I want, we'll call it even."

"I think I can handle that."

And instead of climbing out of my car and heading into my house, I leaned over the center console to give her one last kiss.

READ THE NEXT BOOK IN THIS SERIES:
MEET ME THERE
ASHLYN AND LUKE'S STORY

A dark Chemistry lab. A fake British accent. It's all fun and games until somebody falls in love.

When sixteen-year-old, Ashlyn Brooks, runs into a sweet British guy in the dark Chemistry lab, she has no idea she's actually sitting in the pitch black room with her longtime rival, Luke Davenport. She also doesn't know that she's stepped into another one of the football captain's pranks. It isn't long before she's sharing things she's never told anyone, and starting to fall for the mysterious guy with a sexy accent who seems to understand her in a way no one ever has before.

When Luke's mom dies the summer before his senior year, he turns to pranking Ashlyn to keep his mind off his loss. But the more he gets to know her, the more he regrets using his fake British accent in the first place. Soon Luke is walking the thin line of keeping his lies a secret and wishing he could tell her that the boy she's falling for is really him.

Enjoy this Sneak Peek of MEET ME THERE.

ASHLYN

CHAPTER ONE

Breaking up with Noah was a good thing. I gave my reflection a pep talk one more time before leaving the locker room. *You made the right choice. Life is better without him.*

I drew in a deep breath, trying to calm my first-day-of-school jitters. My blonde hair looked okay after being in a ponytail for this morning's 6:30 a.m. drill team practice. My blue eyes were maybe a little tired looking, but that was to be expected since I'd slept terribly last night. At least my new outfit rocked—an awesome floral printed blouse with dark skinny jeans. It had felt like Christmas when I'd found the last shirt in my size at Chic Girl Boutique. Being a tall girl made it hard to find shirts that fit my long torso just right.

I inspected myself one last time before pulling my bag over my shoulder and leaving the deserted locker room. All the other drill team girls had left five minutes ago, excited to see everyone again after summer break.

I made it to the top of the stairs that led away from the gym, and then scanned the hall. There were different clusters of students standing around, but no Noah.

Good. I breathed a sigh of relief. Last year, when we were still together, he'd always wait for me in the mornings. It was nice he'd decided to change his routine as well. If I was lucky, I might be able to avoid seeing him all morning. Juniors and seniors didn't usually have many classes together, so if I could figure out a way to avoid him at lunch I wouldn't have to see him at all.

I was walking into the main hall when I saw a poster that made my stomach drop.

No!

I rushed forward and ripped the paper from the wall. There was only one person in this school who would do something like this.

I'm going to kill him. I'm going to kill Luke Davenport.

I stared at the flyer. There was a hand-drawn

picture that I assumed was supposed to look like me, since my name stood out in big, bold letters right above it. It looked like a seven-year-old's art project.

BOYFRIEND WANTED

For: Ashlyn Brooks
Junior. 5'8"ish. Dancer. Blonde hair. Blue or Green Eyes. (I think)

He was starting this up again? I shook my head and read over the headline once more. He didn't even do his research before posting the ridiculous thing. I was five-foot-nine and my eyes were most definitely blue. No, I didn't have one green eye and one blue eye like this hideous portrait suggested—something he might notice if he ever took the time to actually look at me instead of pulling these annoying pranks.

But he'd been pulling pranks like this since last spring. It all started when he slipped extra baking soda in my cake during Foods class—and all because I grabbed the last non-flowery apron, leaving him to look like a field of daisies exploded all over his front. One prank led to another, and before long, we were in a war—a friendly war, anyway. I thought he'd forget about our rivalry over the summer, but apparently, he still had nothing better to do with his time. We'd always kept our pranks fairly harmless, but this...this was going too far. How long had these flyers been up? And how many people had seen them? Had Noah seen them and thought *I* had posted them? I was going to throw up.

I read the rest of the flyer.

Seeking guys with the following qualifications:

Happy to commit. (Good ol' ball and chain.)

Loves to pamper his girl.

Tall, dark, and handsome preferred, but short and squatty are OK.

Must love shopping for hours at Chic Girl Boutique.

Must be fine with watching chick flicks over football.

If interested, call Ashlyn at 315-555-7892

Or wait for me by my black Mercedes after school for your interview.

My jaw dropped. He actually put my real number on there. I crumpled the flyer in a ball and looked down the hall bustling with students. There were identical ads taped on lockers all along the row. My face flushed with heat as I rushed down the tiled floor, knowing I only had a couple of minutes before the bell rang. I didn't want to be late for my first class. I ripped down sign after sign, going down the main hall as fast as I could in three-inch wedges.

The warning bell rang.

No!

I made one mad dash, ripping the last flyer down before the hall was completely full of students rushing to their first-period classes. I threw the offending flyers in the trash and headed to my locker to grab my History notebook.

My friend and next-door neighbor, Eliana, saw me as soon as I turned the corner.

"Did you see them?" Eliana asked in a hushed tone, her blue eyes searching mine for signs of a freak-out.

I nodded. "Just barely. I took down as many as I could on my way here."

"Me too. Your brother and I started yanking them down as soon as we got here, but we could only get the ones in this hall."

I opened my locker, resisting the urge to punch it. "Why does Luke keep doing this? Doesn't he have anyone else he can annoy?"

Eliana leaned her barely five-foot frame against her locker, her notebooks hugged to her chest. Her dad was from Italy and her mom was from here, so she looked gorgeous with her darker features and light eyes. "I have no idea, but we definitely need to get him back good this time."

"For real." He'd taken these pranks to a new level of public humiliation. He needed some public humiliation himself.

My brother Jess walked up behind us then. "Do you want me to take care of Luke this time?" he asked in his protective, older-brother voice.

"No. You don't need to get involved. But I'm open to suggestions for revenge."

Jess checked his watch. "The late bell is gonna ring in a minute, but we'll talk more about this after school." He looked at Eliana. "See you at Math Club?"

She nodded, and then Jess left us.

"You guys have Math Club on the first day of school?"

Eliana shrugged. "Not officially. But since Jess and I are in charge this year, he figured we should go over some stuff with Miss Maloney today if we could."

I couldn't keep a grin from spreading across my cheeks. "You guys are such nerds."

"And proud of it!" She grinned back. "Anyway, I

better get to class. But I'll grab any flyers I see on my way. Sorry about this. Luke went overboard this time."

I was almost to my History classroom when I spotted the devil himself. Luke was leaning against the wall as if he'd been waiting for me to walk by. It wouldn't surprise me if he'd stolen my class schedule from the office. When our eyes met, a smirk lifted his lips. He pushed himself off the wall and his long legs fell into step next to mine.

"How's your first day going?" he asked.

"Fabulously," I said, my voice dripping with sarcasm. "Pretty much a dream. I've always wanted to see a cartoon version of my face plastered all over the school. Did you draw that picture yourself?"

He grinned. "No, actually my neighbor was selling her art on the sidewalk last weekend and her picture reminded me so much of you I had to buy it."

I wanted to smack that smug look off his face. How could a guy who looked so cute and innocent be so devious? It wasn't fair. Guys should come with a warning label. I mean, I could've saved myself a lot of trouble last year if Noah's cover had matched his inside.

"It was great to see you again as always, Luke," I

said when we reached my destination. "Oh, and my eyes are blue, for future reference."

He stopped and peered into my eyes for a moment, his own brown ones catching me by surprise. Had they always had that much gold mixed in with them?

"Ah, yes, blue," he said, his warm minty breath tickling my face. "I'll have to tell my neighbor so she can get it right next time. You wouldn't happen to know what your blood type is, would you?"

My stomach lurched. "My blood type?"

The smirk was back on his lips. "Totally joking there."

I slugged him in the arm—a very well-defined arm. No wonder he was the football captain this year. He probably worked out in all of his free time to get so sculpted. He definitely hadn't been so big last spring. He seemed taller as well. He had to be at least six-two or six-three.

I shook my head, hoping he hadn't noticed my lingering gaze. He was still rubbing his arm where I'd hit him. That made me smile. Who says dancers aren't tough? "You better hurry to your class before the bell rings. I'll look forward to planning our next meeting."

He raised an eyebrow. "By 'meeting,' you mean your next form of revenge?"

"Of course."

His grin spread wider. For some reason, one I couldn't understand, Luke seemed to be looking forward to my participation in the pranking game again.

Deciding I'd have to figure him out later, I turned on my heel to find my seat in U.S. History.

My phone buzzed in my pocket. There were about a dozen missed text messages and five missed calls, all from numbers I didn't recognize.

315-555-2934: **UR hot. I'll be your boyfriend.**

315-555-2345: **I'll dump my girlfriend 4 you.**

315-555-9723: **meet me in the maintenance closet @ lunch 4 a good time.**

The rest of the texts were along the same lines. Who in their right mind would think I'd be interested in any of those things? Oh yeah, guys who thought the ad was actually real.

I'm going to kill Luke Davenport.

I was barely able to concentrate on my classes the

rest of the morning because I kept getting texts. Most of them were from total idiots, but there were a few that seemed sincere. Had every guy at school seen the ads? There couldn't be that many guys interested in dating me. It's not like I was that popular. Maybe Luke put all his friends up to this. I wouldn't put it past him. I mean, no guy in their right mind would actually be interested in filling the "boyfriend wanted" spot, given those outrageous requirements on the flyer.

If my phone was this popular during class, what the heck was I supposed to do during lunch? Jess and Eliana's meeting would probably take forever. And without them, I didn't have anyone else to hang out with since I'd always been with Noah. If I sat at a table by myself, Luke's buddies might try "helping" his plan along even further.

The bell rang, and I fully planned to join Jess and Eliana in their meeting today. I could pretend to be a Mathlete. It might be kind of nice to have built-in tutors everywhere.

I took my time packing up my things from Ceramics. If I waited in here for a few minutes, then I wouldn't have to run into Noah during lunch.

But Noah must have had the same idea because when I stepped out into the hall, I came face to face with my ex for the first time since our breakup. My breath caught in my throat. He looked even better than he had when we were dating. And not seeing him in two months hadn't changed anything about my body's reaction to him. He still had the same dark brooding brown eyes and auburn hair with a slight curl in it.

He seemed to take in my appearance as well, and I couldn't help but wonder what he thought about seeing me again.

"Saw your boyfriend-wanted posters this morning," he said in his deep, gravelly voice. "Having a hard time getting along without me?"

I flushed, my brain scrambling for a response. "I didn't put those flyers up."

He crossed his arms and chuckled. "Yeah, well, if anybody tries to fill the ad, I'll tell them not to waste their time."

My eyes instantly burned at his words and the memories they evoked. I had put up with so much while we dated, and now I was a waste of time?

I pinched my eyes shut and sucked in a quick breath, willing the tears to stay inside. I couldn't let Noah know his words had any effect on me. He didn't deserve to have that kind of power over me anymore.

"Goodbye, Noah." I whirled around and walked

away, knowing I wouldn't be able to keep the tears at bay for much longer.

"See ya."

While Luke Davenport was mostly annoying, Noah Taylor was the bad habit I'd broken too late.

LUKE

"Thank you, Mr. Sawyer, for never locking this room," I whispered under my breath as I slipped into the dark Chemistry lab and sat down on the floor beside the door. I felt like a coward hiding in here during lunch, but I was going to explode if one more stranger came up and told me how sorry they were to hear about my mom dying this summer. Sure, posting those "boyfriend wanted" posters for Ashlyn had distracted everyone for a while, but apparently, our school counselor thought I was "acting out." And to help me "grieve" in a more appropriate way, she had rallied a committee of do-gooders to try and cheer me up.

But I didn't need a bunch of girls looking at me

with their sad, pitying eyes, trying to get me to talk about my "feelings." These pranks had been awesome last year when my mom was sick, why shouldn't they help me now?

My stomach growled, reminding me it was there. I smothered it with my arms.

Just a few more minutes and I could sneak out to my Jeep to grab some lunch.

I was about to stand when the door opened, and someone tripped over my sprawled legs.

Oof!

"Sorry!" a female voice squealed as she landed on me.

A girl? Had one of those do-gooders followed me here? How many people had the school counselor told?

I tried to help the girl get up, but it was so dark and there were no windows here—our heads crashed together instead.

"Ouch!" she said.

"Sorry." I rubbed my forehead where our skulls had collided.

We righted ourselves, and I leaned back against the wall of cupboards behind us. She scooted a few feet away.

We sat in silence for a few moments until I heard her sniffling like she was trying not to cry.

"Are you okay? Did my head hurt you?" She sniffled again, so I asked, "Are you crying?"

"No," she said, her voice uneven. "I'm just hiding from a stupid jerk."

There was something familiar about her voice.

I couldn't have everyone at school knowing the football captain hid in the Chemistry lab during lunch, so I lowered my voice, just in case this was someone I knew. "Who's the jerk?"

Okay, it sounded like I had a bad cold, but hopefully, I hadn't said enough earlier for her to notice the difference. Was it too late to start using my fake British accent? I was excellent at impersonations. Random talent, but it did come in handy sometimes.

"Nobody important," she said.

Okay, so some dude made her cry. She probably wouldn't want to be in the same room as me after hearing what I'd done that morning. Luckily for me though, Ashlyn hadn't cried. She was too mad to do that. Boy, was I going to be in trouble once she figured out how to get me back. She always came back with something strong.

"If it makes you feel better, I think he's a jerk too."

I tried to make it sound like I was joking, but somehow my fake British accent slipped out when I said those words. Oh well, not like it mattered. We were sitting in the dark, and I'd be leaving soon anyway.

She laughed, and I felt like I'd been hit by a sack of rocks. I knew that laugh. I'd heard that sweet melodic sound about a billion times last year in Foods class.

This girl was Ashlyn Brooks.

Crap! My stomach shrunk in on itself. Had she been crying because of my prank this morning? She'd seemed fine when I talked to her. Maybe her tears were because of my friends' texts? I'd told them to keep it clean—to just have fun with her. But I should have realized that was impossible. Kellen and Jake had a few too many concussions to follow my directions very well.

"You don't even know which jerk I'm talking about." She laughed again.

Oh, but I did. She was talking about me. I needed to get out of there before she figured out who I was. I snuck a peek in her direction and was grateful I could barely make out her silhouette. If I couldn't pick out much about her, then hopefully she couldn't see much of me. I moved my leg closer to the sliver of light coming from under the door, just in case.

"Sorry about tripping over you," she said like she still had no idea who I was.

I cleared my throat and focused on maintaining my British accent. "Sorry about blocking the door." *Okay, Luke, it's time to leave now. You're pushing your luck every second you stay in here.*

But my legs seemed to be frozen to the tiled floor. Plus, if I did leave, I'd have to open the door and the light would give away who I was. And then she would hate me even more for disguising my voice. So I sat there.

"Are you from England or something?"

Definitely *or something.* "Uh, yeah. I moved here over the summer."

"What part of England?" she asked like she thought it was so cool. Or hot. My ex-girlfriend always said my impression of a British guy was sexy.

"I'm from London."

"That's so cool! I've always wanted to visit."

"You should. It's nice...and overcast?" *You're an idiot, Luke.* I needed to stop pretending like I knew anything about England when the extent of my knowledge came from the *Pride and Prejudice*-type movies my mom had me watch with her when she was sick.

"Is it weird that I want to sit in the dark for a while longer?" she asked.

"Depends."

"Depends on what?"

"Depends on whether you think it's weird that I want to stay in here too." Which was so strange because it was true. Ashlyn and I were supposed to be sworn rivals.

She laughed. Maybe that was a good sign? I heard her shift on the tile floor like she was getting comfortable.

"What were you doing sitting here in the dark anyway?" she asked.

I bit my lip, trying to decide if I wanted to tell her the truth or not. There was something about the anonymity that made me feel like I could tell her anything. Here in the dark, I could be anyone.

I could be myself.

Or at least my real self who also happened to have a British accent and a really deep voice.

"I was hiding," I said.

"Hiding from who?"

Reality.

I shook my head. "Doesn't matter. I just need to lay low for a few minutes."

"Looks like neither one of us wants to say much about why we're in here," she said. "I guess I better get going anyway."

"Wait!" I said, surprising myself.

She seemed to startle. "Why?"

"Because I-I still don't know anything about you," I lied. Why was I doing this? I should be relieved she wanted to go, not suddenly interested in getting to know Ashlyn better.

I expected her to stand. But she didn't. "What do you want to know?" she asked in a soft voice.

I thought about it. "Hmmm. It's kind of fun not knowing who I'm talking to, so let's set up some rules."

"Rules?"

I smiled, though I knew she couldn't see it. "Yes, rules. This is likely the only opportunity we'll ever have to get to know someone without seeing them first. It's like the ultimate clean slate, aside from the fact that I know you're a girl, and you know I'm a guy."

"And that you're from England."

Right.

I continued, "We should make a rule that we can only speak the truth in here. No saying something just because we think that's what people want to hear. Wouldn't it be nice to get to know someone with all the walls down?" The irony of my whole honesty comment was not lost on me as I used my fake accent.

She was quiet for a moment. Then she said, "That would be nice. There're no pre-judgments based on looks, reputation, or anything. We can get to know the real us." I heard a smile in her voice. "I kind of like that idea."

"Good." I found myself smiling as well. "So, tell me about yourself, Mystery Girl. Tell me things you don't tell anyone else."

"Mystery Girl?" She laughed. "I'm not that interesting."

"Oh, but you are. I'm already intrigued." What could Ashlyn Brooks darkest secrets be?

She laughed again. "Are we talking surface-level stuff or deep stuff?"

"I'm tired of the surface level. That's all anyone wants to hear these days. Let's go scuba diving."

"Scuba diving?" Her voice was covered in disbelief. "Are you sure?"

"Definitely."

"Okay, you asked for it," she said in a low voice.

She was quiet for a long time, but then she let out a tiny giggle. "I really, really like the color blue. Like, every time I'm outside I look at the sky and sigh."

What? "Are you for real?"

It sounded like her shoulders were shaking against the cupboards, almost as if she was suppressing her laughter. "Sorry, I had to. Things were way too serious in here."

I shook my head and smiled at this version of Ashlyn that I'd never known was there.

"How about I go first then," I said. But as soon as I said that, I had nothing interesting to say. Nothing that would fit this *all-important moment* of finally letting someone know who Luke Davenport was beneath all the layers and masks...and fake accents.

"It's harder than you thought, huh?" she said, seeming to understand my hesitation.

"Yeah." I sighed. "The only thing I could come up with was that my favorite food is pizza."

More laughter from her. *Score!* Maybe scuba diving wasn't that important anyway. She'd been on the verge of crying when she first came in here... because of me...and now she was laughing...also because of me. If anything, that made this interaction a success.

Her phone buzzed from inside her bag, and she

pulled it out. The screen lit up, which let me see her profile better: Perfectly straight nose. Full lips. Dainty chin. Yep, it was definitely Ashlyn.

She groaned, and then said, "I better go. Maybe we should try telling our deepest darkest secrets again sometime."

My breath caught in my throat. Really? She wanted to meet me again? "Yeah, that would be cool. Wanna try again tomorrow? Same time, same place, same lighting?" My pulse throbbed as I waited for her to respond. Who knew the possibility of being rejected by Ashlyn could be so scary?

"I can't tomorrow, but how about Monday?" she said to my relief.

"Monday would be great."

"Okay, I really do need to leave now. Promise you won't look?" she asked.

I smiled. "I'll even wait a few minutes before I come out, for good measure."

She stood, and I moved my legs out of the way so she wouldn't trip over them again. I heard her hand fumbling around before she opened the door. When the light from the hallway poured in, I lifted my backpack in front of my face in case she glanced back.

The door shut behind her and the room was dark again.

I sighed, leaning my head against the cupboard. I had no idea what I was doing, or if I could even keep this fake British guy act up, but I hoped she'd come back, because that was the first real conversation I'd had since my mom died.

ALSO BY JUDY CORRY

Ridgewater High Series:

When We Began (Cassie and Liam)

Meet Me There (Ashlyn and Luke)

Don't Forget Me (Eliana and Jess)

It Was Always You (Lexi and Noah)

My Second Chance (Juliette and Easton)

My Mistletoe Mix-Up (Raven and Logan)

Forever Yours (Alyssa and Jace)

Protect My Heart (Emma and Arie)

The Billionaire Bachelor (Kate and Drew)

Kissing The Boy Next Door (Wes and Lauren)

ABOUT THE AUTHOR

Judy Corry has been addicted to love stories for as long as she can remember. She reads and writes YA and Clean Romance because she can't get enough of the feeling of falling in love. She graduated from Southern Utah University with a degree in Family Life and Human Development and loves to weave what she learned about the human experience into her stories. She believes in swoon-worthy kisses and happily ever afters.

Judy met her soul mate while in high school, and

married him a few years later. She and her husband are raising four beautiful and crazy children in Southern Utah.

Made in the USA
Coppell, TX
02 May 2020